The Mystery of Hollow Inn

Samantha Wolf Mysteries #1

TARA ELLIS

ISBN: 1494441020
ISBN-13: 978-1494441029

The Mystery of Hollow Inn

Cover Design© Melchelle Designs
http://melchelledesigns.com/

Cover Models: Breanna Dahl and Janae Dahl
Photographer: Tara Ellis Photography

To all of the wonderful stories I read as a child that inspired me to create my own, mystery-filled world.

Samantha Wolf Mysteries

1. The Mystery of Hollow Inn
2. The Secret of Camp Whispering Pines
3. The Beach House Mystery
4. The Heiress of Covington Ranch
5. The Haunting of Eagle Creek Middle School
6. A Mysterious Christmas on Orcas Island

Find these titles at Tara's author page!

www.amazon.com/author/taraellis

CONTENTS

1. HOLLOW INN   1

2. THE LEGEND   13

3. VOICES FROM THE PAST   22

4. A GHOSTLY ENCOUNTER   35

5. SECRETS   41

6. FLORENCE LAKE   47

7. THE JOURNAL   56

8. A POEM   68

9. CABIN IN THE WOODS   74

10. CLUES   83

11. A CONFESSION   92

12. GOLD MINE   103

13. DISCOVERY   113

14. NARROW ESCAPE   120

15. THE INHERITANCE   126

16. GOING HOME   136

1

HOLLOW INN

Sam and Ally step from the bus into the hot summer day and look at the surrounding countryside. "The Rocky Mountains are even bigger than I remember," Sam observes, gazing at the Montana hills with her pale green eyes. The tall twelve-year-old pulls her brown, shoulder length hair back from her round face.

The last time her parents brought her to Montana was years ago for a family reunion, but that was at a lake miles from here. She's never been this deep in the mountains, or in this part of the state.

She turns to her best friend Ally, who's setting their luggage near a bench in front of the small bus depot. Sam is excited to have her along. They've been planning their trip for the past three months. It took a lot of begging, pleading, and promises, but eventually their parents said yes.

"The scenery is the only good thing I can say about the bus ride," Ally answers. "I can't wait until we get to the inn." Running her fingers through her short, unruly red hair, she stretches dramatically before flattening the wrinkles in her shirt. The spunky pre-teen stands a couple of inches shorter than Sam. The freckles that run across the bridge of her nose, combined with her blue eyes, give away her Irish heritage.

Pulling a phone out of her back pocket, Ally turns in circles, holding it up to the sky. "One bar," she announces with disdain. Typing furiously, she quickly sends out messages to her parents and friends, as if the end of the world were looming. They were warned about the lack of cell and computer service out here.

Sam smiles at her friend, remembering how Ally was so eager to make the ten hour trek just this morning. "Oh, don't complain. There are worse things than not having your phone and the trip really wasn't that bad. But I think that a long swim in the lake Aunt Beth told me about sounds wonderful right now!" The heat of the day is starting to fade, but it's still warm enough to cause sweat to bead at the base of her neck.

"Excuse me."

Sam turns quickly to face a handsome young man of about seventeen. He's wearing a dark tank top over bared muscular shoulders, and thick blonde hair outlines his lean features.

"Yes?" she asks uncertainly.

"You must be Samantha Wolf and Alyson Parker?" Cringing at their formal names, the two girls nod simultaneously and he flashes a warm smile. "Hi, my name is Ted Baker," he says, as he turns and begins gathering up their bags.

Sam steps out of his way and notices the Hollow Inn logo on the front of his shirt. "Nice to meet you, Ted," she says politely. "Please just call us Sam and Ally. Everybody does."

"Sure," he agrees, walking around them. "Your Aunt Beth really wanted to come herself, but there was a little problem at the inn this afternoon."

"What kind of problem?" Sam asks. "Is everything okay?"

Ignoring the question, Ted places their bags into the back of an old station wagon idling nearby and opens the rear doors for them. Ally climbs into the air-conditioned vehicle eagerly, but Sam hesitates. She's tempted to call her aunt and confirm the change in plans. Unfortunately, her number is scribbled in a notebook that is packed away in the back of the car and she doesn't want to make Ted feel uncomfortable. Her phone might not even work.

"Hey Ted! How are things at the inn? I heard about the…mishap."

Spinning around, Sam discovers that the voice belongs to an older man that runs the depot. He greeted the bus driver and welcomed everyone when they arrived. Any question about Ted's intentions evaporates, but the comment seems ominous.

"It's just fine, Mr. Harrison. We've got to run. Have a good evening."

The dismissal is clear, but Mr. Harrison lingers, meeting Sam's gaze.

"Come on Sam, your aunt and uncle are waiting," Ted insists.

Breaking away from the steady gaze of Mr. Harrison, Sam is rewarded by another charming smile from Ted. Settling into the back seat next to Ally, she isn't convinced of the sincerity behind it. "So what happened?" she presses, looking at his reflection in the rear view mirror.

"Oh, it's nothing serious, but I'd better let Mrs. Clark explain it to you herself."

The two girls exchange a look as they fasten their seat belts, but refrain from asking more questions about it. It's obvious he doesn't want to tell them.

"So what's your job at the inn, Ted?" Ally inquires as the car pulls away from the depot. The change of topic seems to make him relax and he leans back in his seat.

"I take care of all the odd jobs around the resort," he answers pleasantly. "I guess you can call me the handyman if you want to give me a title."

"How many people are working there now?" Sam asks. "I didn't think my aunt and uncle had hired the full staff yet."

"No, you're right, they haven't. There are plenty of people available for the jobs around here, but unfortunately a lot of the folks in these hills tend to be superstitious. We've talked enough about jobs, though. I hear you're from the west coast. What's it like?"

"Yeah, we're from Washington State," Sam confirms, noting his reluctance to talk about the inn once again. "We live in a really small, quiet town near the ocean. During the summer it's full of tourists and the traffic is a mess. When Aunt Beth invited us here for a visit, we just jumped at the chance. I've only seen pictures of the house, but it looks like a mansion!"

"It is a mansion, actually," Ted explains. "A very old one. It was built over a hundred years ago. The Hollows have always owned it. It's only been since your Uncle Bill bought the place two years ago that it's been used as an inn." It's obvious Ted knows a lot of the local history and enjoys explaining it. "I don't mean to sound negative," he continues. "But I'm not so sure that it will work out for them."

"Why do you say that?" Ally asks. They turn onto a narrow country road and head up into the woods, leaving the small town behind.

"Because…" he trails off, glancing up into the rear view mirror and then looking quickly away. He seems to come to a decision. "Because of the Hollow Legend," he states matter-of-factly.

Sam leans forward from the back seat eagerly. "Ooh, a legend? Is that what you meant by people being superstitious?" Sam is nearly bouncing in the seat with anticipation, and forces herself to be still. Ted is like a timid rabbit. She can tell it won't take much to scare him away from the topic.

"Yeah, that's what fuels all the stories. I guess I just assumed that your aunt already told you about it. Everyone around here knows the story. But I've already said too much, Sam. She must not have wanted to worry you about it. Please don't let her know I told you. I haven't had this job for too long and I would hate to mess it up. I need it for the whole summer."

"Don't worry, Ted," Sam says quickly, feeling a little guilty now. It really seems like he respects her aunt and uncle. "Aunt Beth isn't like that. I'm sure that the only reason she hasn't told me about it is because she doesn't believe it. If she thought it was important, she would have said something. She and Uncle Bill are so excited about this place, it would take a lot more than a silly legend to make them worry."

The paved road gives way to loose gravel and Ted slows the car slightly. Rolling down the window, he produces a bag of sunflower seeds from the glove compartment and turns to face the girls. "Want some?" When Sam and Ally both shake their heads, he shrugs and tosses a handful in his mouth.

The air blowing in through the open window is surprisingly cool. Sam rolls down her own window, breathing in the fresh air tinged with the smell of warm cedar. Pulling some stray hairs across her forehead, she gazes happily at the beautiful scenery rushing past. These woods are different than the ones back home. The trees are bigger and the forest appears denser. Instead of moss hanging off the branches, sweet smelling pine needles cover the dry ground.

Sighing, she leans contently against the door. It's great to be out of school. She hasn't seen her aunt and uncle in almost three years and has been dreaming about this adventure for weeks. Some of her friends don't understand how she can be excited about spending so much time away from her computer and instant messaging. To be honest, her parents only allowed her to have a smart phone since her twelfth birthday, six months ago, and she finds all the drama associated with it stressful.

Ally seems to thrive in the whole social media thing, but Sam often finds herself wishing she could just shut it off, without the fear of everyone thinking she's weird. She can't think of a better vacation than being tucked away deep in the woods without any pressure to text everyone all the time. Now, to top it all off, there's even a legend! Grinning, she turns to Ally and finds her friend frowning at her phone.

"It's gone," Ally says pathetically. "There's NO signal at all, Sam! OMG, I don't know if I can do this."

For a moment, Sam thinks she actually sees tears threatening in her friend's eyes, but then Ally tosses the phone on the seat and crosses her arms over her chest.

"I don't need it, Sam. I don't care. Chelsie

was like, being all stupid anyways. And then Crystal was all agreeing with her and Matt was even posting snaps of their conversation! Can you believe that? He got like, twenty likes in five minutes and *tagged* me in it!"

Sam silently studies her friend, trying to decide if she is joking or not. Sometimes it's hard to tell. Ted is methodically eating his sunflower seeds, but Sam suspects he is listening carefully to their ridiculous conversation.

Ally then turns to Sam with a flourish and stares back at her for a full minute before they both start laughing.

"Maybe Ted can drive us into town tomorrow so you can intervene and prevent the world from falling apart," Sam suggests.

They both laugh even harder.

"No, I think I'll go along with the whole 'I didn't have a choice' option instead and go hide at your aunt's inn. Even if there *is* some big mystery we aren't allowed to talk about and a spooky legend!" Ally directs the last part to Ted, and when he looks at her, she smiles expectantly.

Ted turns back to the road and drives in silence for a few minutes.

"Oh come on, Ted," Sam pleads. "I won't tell Aunt Beth. Don't you think we should know about it if we're going to be staying there?"

"In these woods," he says solemnly, gesturing at the trees surrounding them, "the Hollow Legend is more than just superstition." He glances in the rear view mirror to gaze at the girl seated behind him. The serious look on her face reminds him of the woman who gave him this summer job.

Leaning towards Ally, Sam speaks to her softly. "Aunt Beth *did* seem distracted this morning when I called her from home before we left. She isn't the sort of person to tell people her problems, but I could tell by her voice that something was wrong. I think Ted knows what it is." She thinks of the old mansion, set deep in the woods. A quiver of anticipation crawls down her spine.

"I guess I might as well tell you that it's the legend that keeps people from working for your uncle." Ted continues, unaware of the whispered conversation between the two girls. "Now, after the…uh, accidents, the stories are starting to turn customers away from Hollow Inn, too."

"Well now you *have* to tell us what the legend is," Ally complains.

"Then you can't let on that you know about it," he says, switching on the headlights to push back the gathering darkness. When both Sam and Ally nod eagerly, he clears his throat and the girls settle back in anticipation of the story to come.

2

THE LEGEND

"Okay, so generations ago a gold miner built a mansion for his beautiful bride-to-be," Ted begins. "He thought she should have only the best. His name was Shawn Hollow. The inn was named after him." He pauses long enough to point out a lake far down in a valley below them. The setting sun reflects off the water and rests on the outstretched limbs of the trees lining the shore.

"That's Florence Lake," Ted explains. "Old Shawn named it after his wife. The inn is on the far end, up that side of the mountain. You can ᴗee the lake from there. You'll find that a lot of the landmarks on the Hollow Estate are named after family members, especially their children. Well, all except for their youngest son. Nothing is named for him. There were four boys, altogether."

A question hangs between Sam and Ally. Why was the youngest boy left out? They soon have the answer.

"Joseph Hollow," Ted announces like a carnival barker. "That's whose ghost is supposedly haunting Hollow Inn, and-"

"A ghost!" Sam interrupts. "You can't be serious!"

"There are no such things as ghosts," Ally declares, looking to Sam for confirmation, while nervously biting at her fingernails.

"I know. It sounds crazy." Ted throws the empty sunflower seed wrapper onto the passenger seat. "I thought the same thing when I came to work here. But not anymore."

Sam waits for a punch line, but none is offered. She laughs half-heartedly at the suggestion that Ted might actually believe a ghost roams the halls of Hollow Inn. "And now what do you think?" she jeers.

"Well, I don't really believe in *all* of the haunting that's supposedly happening, but there are some strange things going on," Ted points out. "For instance, sounds that seem to be coming from the walls bother people during the night. A lady who was staying there claimed she was awakened by someone calling her name. When she looked around the room and saw the window open, she thought maybe she'd just heard the wind. But the same thing happened the next night. Only that time, she swore she saw a dark figure looming over her in the moonlight. Needless to say, she left the next morning. Stories like that spread like wildfire around here."

"How do you know that she really saw anything?" Sam asks. "She probably heard the rumors too, and let her imagination get the better of her."

"Maybe," Ted agrees. "But the strange thing is that the room she stayed in was the late Joseph Hollow's bedroom. You can laugh, but I've heard some weird things around the place myself. It's not just the sounds, though. The real reason your aunt couldn't come get you, Sam, is because of the vandalism."

"What!" Sam exclaims.

"Yeah, it's really hurt business. The whispers of a ghost might actually lure some customers in, but the other stuff is definitely running them off. It's senseless stuff. Bushes are cut or pulled up, windows broken, tires on guest cars are slashed and their belongings are disturbed. Nothing too serious, but enough to keep the rumors flying and make people afraid to stay at the inn. I didn't want to talk about it in front of Mr. Harrison. Your aunt asked me not to say anything to you, either. She doesn't want to scare you."

"Well, I think it *does* sound pretty spooky," Ally says quietly. The idea of ghosts doesn't do anything to brighten her outlook on their trip, especially since she can't even call for help. Reaching instinctively for her phone, she looks at Sam, and then at the suddenly threatening woods, before sitting back farther in the seat. Pressing her lips together, Ally shoves the unusable phone deep into her pocket.

Sam pats her friend on the shoulder and tries to give her a reassuring smile. "I'm not going to worry about it, Ally. This all seems like a common story for an old house. As for the vandalism, it's probably the local kids trying to scare people. I hope something is done about it soon, though. I couldn't stand to see Aunt Beth and Uncle Bill lose everything they've put into fixing up the old place."

The car pushes a little harder as they reach the far end of Florence Lake and start up another steep incline. The sun is now only a faint glow on the horizon, below the lake.

"Now," Sam continues, turning back to Ted. "I suppose the legend is about how Joseph Hollow's ghost came to be haunting Hollow Inn?"

"Exactly," Ted confirms, flashing another smile over his shoulder. Spitting the last of the sunflower shells out the open window, he quickly closes it against the cool mountain night air.

"Florence died while giving birth to their fourth child, Joseph. Shawn believed that it was the boy's fault. As a result, Joseph grew up being resented and unfairly treated by his father. When Joseph was sixteen, Mr. Hollow called his four sons together: Christopher, Michael, Thomas and Joseph.

"He told them he was getting to be an old man and had made a new will. The three older boys would be allowed to stay in the house. All of their lives if they wanted to. They would be given a generous monthly allowance, monitored by Mr. Hollow's attorney. Joseph would only receive a small amount of money. Once Shawn died, the kid would be on his own."

"How horrible!" Ally exclaims from the backseat. "How could he be so cruel to his own son?"

Ted puts his hand up to stop her. "It may have been a low thing to do, Ally, but Joseph didn't exactly have a reputation for being the ideal son, either."

"What do you mean?" Sam asks.

"It's said that Joseph was a troublemaker from day one. He enjoyed causing mischief and problems for everyone around him. He would go into the garden and pull up plants or break dishes in the kitchen, as well as other things, on purpose. Some people thought that Shawn Hollow planned to write him out of his will because he was afraid of him."

"Well, who could blame Joseph?" Ally

protests. "How was he expected to act, knowing how his father felt about him?" She couldn't imagine what it would feel like to know that your own father didn't love you.

"The only thing people saw was a young boy who couldn't control his temper," Ted tries to explain.

Sam quickly makes the connection. "So that's why everyone thinks he's to blame for the vandalism around the mansion."

"But I thought that he was thrown out of the house?" Ally questions, a confused look on her face. "Don't ghosts haunt the places where they die?"

"The will was never carried out," Ted continues. "The very same night that old Shawn announced his intentions, he died in his sleep. The new will he promised was never found. He was a miserly man, and it was no secret that he didn't trust anyone but himself with his money. The four boys knew that Shawn hid most of his earnings somewhere in the mansion. They were bound and determined to find it.

"Now, Joseph's three older brothers were just as greedy as their father had been. They didn't plan on sharing the money with a younger brother who was never meant to have it.

"About a week after Shawn died, Joseph's body was found in Florence Lake. His boat was overturned. The sheriff was satisfied with the explanation that Joseph accidentally drowned, although everyone knew that he was an excellent swimmer.

"As far as I know," Ted finishes, "according to the townspeople, the other three boys grew old in the house. They were basically hermits, obsessed with finding the money. They never did, though, and they blamed their failure on Joseph. They said that he kept them from it. They believed Joseph's ghost would stay there forever, guarding the money that he felt belonged to him and driving off anyone who tried to take the house away. In the end, he finally got the place all to himself, even if he *was* only a ghost. That's it. That's how it all began."

As they continue through the woods, the night wins its battle and closes around them. Occasionally, the headlights expose the glowing eyes of small animals. Over the next crest, the outline of the large mansion comes into view. A full moon is already working its way up the sky behind them, illuminating the tips of the tallest trees and casting shadows where there wouldn't normally be any. There is no mistaking the structure for anything but Hollow Inn, and Ted turns the station wagon up the long driveway.

"The story might be convincing," Sam says out of the darkness, "but I don't believe in ghosts. If there is something strange going on at Hollow Inn, I'm going to find out what it is."

3

"You two must be exhausted!"

A short, rather plump woman in her mid-forties embraces the young girls at the front door. After taking off an apron covering her summer dress, she brushes a stray hair from her face. "How was your trip?" she asks, looking from one girl to the other. "I hope it wasn't too long. I know it isn't your idea of a fun day!"

"It was fine, Aunt Beth," Sam assures her, after returning the hug.

They stand in a large entry way at the bottom

of massive oak stairs that blend into the hardwood floor. To the left is an old, ornate desk set up against the wall. On top of it sits a fancy guest book for people to sign. Beyond it is an arched entrance to a grand room, and Sam can see glimpses of dark, antique furniture facing a large bay window. She can only imagine the view from there in the daylight.

"The scenery on the way up was wonderful!" Sam continues, still looking around. To the right, mouth-watering smells drift through slatted double doors which have to lead to the kitchen. "Ted kept us entertained on the drive here." Glancing over at the blushing man still holding their bags, she smiles.

"What she means," Ally quickly explains, "is that he told us some funny stories about the people around here."

Beth looks skeptically at Ted for a moment, but lets it go. "Thank you for getting the girls, Ted. You're a lifesaver," she says warmly, taking the luggage from him. She lifts the bags with ease, revealing that perhaps the plumpness is misleading.

Ted nods politely and heads back out the

door. "You're welcome, Mrs. Clark. It was my pleasure. I've really got to go now, though. I still have some things to do before turning in tonight." He waves goodbye and then closes the door behind him.

"So, obviously, you're Ally," Beth says, setting the bags at the foot of the stairs. "Sam has told me enough about you that I think I could pick you out of a crowd!" Smiling, she clasps Ally's hands, and her positive energy is contagious.

Ally nods in confirmation, thinking that maybe it really won't be so bad out here after all.

"Sorry about the lack of cell service," Beth says to them both, as if reading Ally's mind. "They've been telling us for the past year that it will improve, but so far it hasn't happened. We have internet access, but it's on a dial-up modem and patchy. We're the last house on a private road, so we aren't exactly at the top of the list for extended services. Most guests don't seem to mind, though. They come here expecting to escape the stress of daily life and actually enjoy not being available at the drop of a hat.

"Down the hall is a phone that you're

welcome to use anytime." She points to a narrow hall past the stairs. "I'm sure your parents would like to know you got here safely, so why don't you go call them now while I dish up some food? I prepared a late dinner for you."

Sam's stomach grumbles at the thought of eating, and she realizes just how hungry she is. "Thanks, Aunt Beth! I forgot to call before we left the bus station, so I'm sure Mom is waiting to hear from us."

After the girls place quick calls to home, they join Beth in the big country kitchen. In contrast to the warm, dark colors of the main house, this area is bright and cheery. It's obvious that the kitchen was recently remodeled. While still charming, it lacks the old, antique feel of the foyer.

"Welcome to *my* room," Beth says happily. She stands at a large butcher-top table at the far end. "We wanted to keep the old charm of the inn, but I refused to work in a hundred-year-old kitchen! Besides," she adds, placing bowls of delicious looking stew in front of them, "I love all that wood, but a kitchen needs to be…light. You know, a place that energizes you and makes you want to run around!" Laughing at herself, she scoops out a third bowl. "I ate earlier, but this smells so good that I think I'm going to have seconds!"

Sam and Ally eagerly sit down and start eating while Beth adds fresh rolls to the meal and pours glasses of milk. She then joins them, talking in between mouthfuls, waving a roll in the air. "Don't worry about your bags. Your Uncle Bill can take them up to your rooms later when he gets here. He wasn't able to meet you because he had to go to a town in the opposite direction.

"As you've seen, we are quite remote here. The two closest towns are almost an hour's drive. The bus depot is in Jackson, which doesn't have much more than the depot, post office, bar and church. Bill had to go to Sunnydale, where they have several stores, to get some special fixtures. We're still in the process of doing some remodeling," she adds hastily, looking down at her bowl.

"Oh…Mr. Harrison at the depot said something about a 'mishap' here. Is everything okay?" Sam asks innocently.

Putting her spoon down, Beth studies her

niece for a moment. "That Mr. Harrison is a busybody," she finally says, her food forgotten. "It was nothing, just some local kids jumping on the legend bandwagon."

"Legend?" Ally asks hesitantly, looking guiltily at Sam. It's not like they're lying, but neither girl feels right about misleading their host.

"Please," Beth states, smiling again. "Don't try to tell me that Ted didn't give you all the details on the way here."

When Sam starts to deny it, Beth holds up a hand. "I've been around awhile, Sam. Long enough to know how to read people. Don't worry about it," she continues, seeing the look of concern on Sam's face. "I don't mind. You would have heard about it eventually. Kinda hard to avoid it out here. It's just a bunch of folklore anyways. I don't put much merit in it. There have been some unexplained occurrences, but certainly nothing that I would say a *ghost* is capable of. Regardless of which it is, though, ghosts or kids, it still upsets paying guests."

"What sort of things have been happening, Mrs. Clark?" Ally asks tentatively.

"Ally, please call me Aunt Beth. And it's just

some mindless vandalism around the grounds. Visitors get spooked over little things. An old house makes a lot of noise, but fueled by the legend, it becomes whispering ghosts as far as the guests are concerned."

"What I don't understand," Sam says, "is how anyone can know the story in such detail when it happened so long ago. Do you think any of it is even true?"

"Well, it's only been ten years since Mr. Hollow's last son died. No one lived here since then, and everyone says it's because the place has such a strange reputation. No one wanted to buy it. Ten years isn't very long, though. As for knowing the distant past, the realtors we bought the house from said they found Shawn Hollow's journal when they cleaned up the place. The three boys passed on the stories from that book themselves, telling how it all began."

"Do you have the journal?" Sam asks with excitement. "Can we see it?"

Beth laughs at her niece's enthusiasm. "Sure, Sam. I'll try to find it." Placing her empty bowl in the dishwasher, she looks at the ceiling. "I think it's in one of the old trunks in the attic."

Sam is surprised when her aunt walks briskly from the room. She didn't expect her to go look for it right now.

"Your Aunt Beth is really nice," Ally says, watching her leave. "I hope she isn't just pretending not to be mad."

"No, if she were mad, she would say so. Aunt Beth doesn't mess around that way. She'll let you know what she's thinking. I found that out at a young age." Smiling now, Sam finishes the last bite of stew and adds her bowl to the washer. "Just don't break something and try to hide it. That makes her really mad."

Ally laughs at this and helps Sam finish clean up the dinner. By the time they figure out where things go, they hear Beth coming back down the stairs. Moments later, she reappears through the swinging kitchen doors, holding a large hardcover book in the crook of her arm. Its yellowing pages are visible between the worn covers.

"Here it is!" Beth exclaims. "It was right on top of the second chest I opened. Read all you like, girls. You'll probably find it quite entertaining. I haven't read it myself, but Shawn Hollow was said to be a fine writer."

Sam carefully takes the book from her aunt and randomly picks a page to read out loud.

"July 19, 1925 Today Florence went into labor with our fourth child. I've sent Christopher for Doctor Suthers. He should return by morning. It's different this time. The pain seems to be worse and Miss Nancy can't keep dear Florence calm. It's almost as if the baby is fighting her."

Sam says nothing, but turns eagerly to the next entry.

"July 20, 1925 Florence died this morning. Christopher returned by dawn, as I expected, but the doctor arrived too late. From her death I acquired a son, but I can't possibly love someone who killed the only person in my life who loved me back."

"My," Aunt Beth exhales. "That certainly is a sad story, for both Shawn and Joseph. It wasn't the boy's fault, but I sympathize with how Shawn must have felt in that moment."

"You really haven't read this, Aunt Beth?" Sam asks, surprised. "I thought that's how you know so much."

"No, I've only skimmed over a few pages. I think the only person to read the whole thing was Thomas Hollow. He was the last son that lived here. He died ten years ago, in 2003, and was the one who found the journal. He told the stories, and they've continued to be passed on. I imagine they've been changed a bit in order to suit the imaginations of paranoid neighbors."

The doors to the kitchen open again and a tall older man with slightly graying hair steps into the room.

"Uncle Bill!" Sam exclaims, jumping from her chair.

Mr. Clark sets down his bag of groceries and embraces his niece, then steps back. "Look at you!" he says, surprised. "You've grown up so much over the last three years!"

Sam grins at her uncle, and introduces Ally before sitting back down.

"Welcome to Hollow Inn," Uncle Bill says to them both. "We're sure glad that you were able to come."

Ted appears behind Bill, loaded down with more bags of groceries. He sets them on the counter and then quietly excuses himself.

While unloading the bags and putting away the food, Uncle Bill notices the journal sitting out on the table. "What's this?" he asks, raising his eyebrows at Beth.

"The girls were curious about the inn's past." She quickly closes the book.

"All that legend stuff is a lot of hogwash," he says, scowling. "There's no such thing as ghosts." He promptly changes the subject. "Where are the Andersons and that Steve fellow?"

"Mr. Smith was scheduled to leave this afternoon, and the Andersons decided to…check out early," Beth finishes, glancing at the girls.

"What do you mean, 'check out early'?" Bill doesn't pick up on the subtle hint to let it go. "I thought they were paid up until next week?"

"Well, you know how things go," Beth explains, wringing her hands nervously. "Plans change."

Bill starts to ask another question, but a more obvious look from Beth silences him.

"You mean you don't have *anyone* staying on this whole estate right now?" Sam asks, now understanding the seriousness of the situation. It's summertime. The rooms should be full.

"No," her aunt admits hesitantly. "No one except for the hired help, of course."

"Now, Sam," Bill says, heading back out of the kitchen. "You wipe that look off your face.

Beth and I don't want you worrying about us having enough customers. We're doing just fine. I'll get your bags and show you two to your rooms. Lord knows we've got plenty to choose from!"

Sam and Ally say goodnight to Aunt Beth and go out to the entry hall where Bill has already started up the creaky stairs with their belongings. At the top, the hallway branches off in both directions. They turn to the right, passing several closed doors.

"I hope you like the rooms," he says, as they finally stop towards the end of the long hall that runs the length of the house on the second floor. "There's a connecting door between you, and if you need anything just dial zero on the phone. It's an intercom, too, so you can speak directly with us in our room and in the kitchen." He tells them both goodnight and heads back down the stairs.

Sam and Ally let themselves in and marvel at the large rooms, decorated with antiques. After briefly running around and inspecting everything, they choose which one they want, and then admit how tired they are. Even though it's barely eleven, they say goodnight and get ready for bed.

As Sam slides under the covers of her huge, old-fashioned four-poster bed, silence settles over Hollow Inn. Although she can barely keep her eyes open, she can't resist the journal that she brought upstairs with her.

Propping herself up with multiple pillows, Sam places the book in her lap and stares at the front cover. She tries to imagine what it would have been like to sit in the same room ninety years ago. "What were Joseph and Shawn like?" she asks herself out loud. *Maybe,* she thinks, *this journal will tell me.* But fatigue sets in quickly and she soon finds the handwritten words blurring. After reading the first line over again three times, she realizes the diary will have to wait until morning. "I guess I'm sleepier than I thought," she admits to the empty room.

She sets the heavy book on the nightstand and clicks off the lamp. Shadows swallow the room, having already claimed the rest of the inn, and the full moon sends streaks of silver through the thin curtains. With thoughts of Shawn and Joseph Hollow dancing through her mind, Sam is soon fast asleep.

4

A GHOSTLY ENCOUNTER

A soft thud. A light scraping sound of wood against wood. Another soft thud. Is she dreaming? Sam tries to pull herself up through heavy webs of sleep. Another unmistakable sound: someone breathing close to her head. Now she comes fully awake with a start.

"Who's there?" she cries out, her voice a hoarse croak. Trying desperately to rub the sleep from her eyes, she pushes herself up against the headboard.

Swallowing a knot of rising panic that

threatens to overtake her, she searches the thick darkness as her eyes adjust. At last, she makes out a dark shape moving ever so slightly, as if trying to quietly back away from the bed without being spotted.

Paralyzed with fear, Sam blinks rapidly, hoping that her mind is seeing something that isn't really there. *It's just my imagination…it's just my imagination*, she murmurs to herself. Her heartbeat hammers in her head so loudly she can't hear anything else. Holding her breath, she waits…there! Yes, there is definitely someone moving near the foot of the bed!

When she hears the same undeniable scraping sound as before, it breaks through the paralysis. Lunging for the bedside lamp, Sam cries out her uncle's name without even realizing it.

"Bill! Bill! Uncle Bill!" Her screams of terror echo down the halls as her fingers curl around the lamp's string. She pulls it frantically, squinting against the sudden flood of light. Spinning back to face the foot of the bed…Sam finds absolutely nothing!

The door to her room slams open and Bill

stands in the doorway, his breaths coming in ragged gasps. Beth soon appears behind him, her face a mixture of concern and fear. Then the pounding starts.

"Sam! Sam, open the door!" Ally's worried shouts come from the other side of their connecting door. "Open the door, Sam! Sam!"

Bill walks quickly across the room, looking around him as he goes. Beth rushes to Sam's side, taking her niece by the shoulders. Before Beth has a chance to ask any questions, Bill releases the lock and Ally nearly falls through the entrance.

"Sam, you're OK!" Ally exclaims, throwing herself at her friend and embracing her.

"What in tarnation happened in here?" Bill asks, seating himself on the edge of the bed.

"I'm sorry," Sam apologizes. "I didn't mean to scream, it just came out. There was someone...or *something* in my room."

"What?" Beth gasps.

Ally's freckles stand out a bit more as the color drains from her face. She resumes biting her nails.

"Who was here?" Bill asks logically. "Where

did they go? I didn't pass anyone in the hall."

"I don't know," Sam admits. "Some noises woke me up. A figure was standing by the bed, trying to back away slowly so I wouldn't see it in the dark. When I finally got my senses about me and turned on the light, it was gone." For some reason, Sam looks over at the nightstand and feels relief at the sight of the journal still lying there.

"I don't like this," Beth says, gripping Sam's hand tightly. "I should have never had you two come out here with all the problems we've been having. Maybe you should go back home tomorrow and come visit us later, when things settle down."

"Oh, no!" Sam exclaims, alarmed. "Please don't make us go home, Aunt Beth. I'm fine. Really. Maybe I was just dreaming, what with all the talk about ghosts right before we went to bed. I do get bad nightmares sometimes."

"Sam is right, Beth," Bill says reassuringly. "Nobody was hurt. If anyone was in the room, I would have seen them. If Sam and Ally want to stay, I don't see any harm in it."

Beth doesn't look convinced, but nods her

head in agreement anyways. "Do you want to stay, Ally?" she asks, looking now at the frightened girl.

Ally glances back and forth between Sam and Beth, and then shrugs. "Sure, why not," she says with a confidence she doesn't feel.

"Okay, then," Bill says decisively, slapping the tops of his thighs. "You stay. Maybe you should sleep in here with Sam tonight, though."

"Sure!" Ally agrees eagerly, already jumping under the covers. She doesn't need any coaxing.

"Are you sure you're okay, Sam?" Beth persists, as she stands to go. "You seemed so scared. I feel horrible about this."

"I'm fine, Aunt Beth. You know what an active imagination I have. I just had a dream and was slow to wake up."

"Come on, Beth," Bill says, reassuring her. "Let's let them get some sleep. If they have any problems, I'm sure they'll holler." Grinning now, he tells the girls goodnight and ushers Beth from the room, closing the door behind them.

Sam and Ally sit for a moment, looking at each other.

"Do you really think it was a dream?" Ally

asks quietly.

Sam slowly shakes her head back and forth.

Ally swallows, looking around the room. "Why not?" she finally asks.

"Because," Sam explains, "I didn't lock that connecting door."

5

SECRETS

The second day of their vacation greets Sam and Ally with a warm morning full of birdsong. Sam showers and dresses quickly in a pair of cut-offs and a light, bright red t-shirt. Drying her long hair vigorously with a towel, she walks into the adjoining room, where Ally is seated at an antique vanity.

"How does Florence Lake sound?" Sam asks happily, trying to forget the night before.

"It sounds like a good idea," Ally replies, applying some lip gloss. She turns on the old swivel stool, and looks at Sam solemnly.

"Don't look at me like that," Sam says. "I'm sure there's nothing to worry about. I just don't want Aunt Beth to send us home. If she knew that wasn't a dream I had last night, we'd be on the first bus out of here."

"I know," Ally replies. "It's just that I feel like we're deceiving your aunt. I guess there's no real harm in it, though." Sighing, she makes up her mind and jumps up from the chair. "Let's try to pretend like the whole thing never happened, and have some fun."

"That's what I want to hear!" Sam exclaims as they head for the door.

The two girls descend the staircase, following the delicious aroma of bacon and eggs cooking. They quicken their pace and enter the kitchen, now filled with morning sunshine. Aunt Beth is standing over the stove, making breakfast.

"Good morning, girls!" Beth says cheerfully, dishing up the eggs. "How did you sleep the rest of the night?"

"I slept great, Aunt Beth," Sam answers as she sits down. After sampling some of the bacon, Sam realizes someone is missing. "Where's Uncle Bill?"

"He had to go back into town. We need some new lights for the walk outside." Beth explains as she sits beside Sam and takes a long swallow of juice.

"Why didn't he get them last night?" Ally asks.

"Because they weren't needed then," Sam says firmly. "I couldn't help but notice the lights on the way in last night, there are so many along the front walk. They seemed to be working fine then. What happened, Aunt Beth?"

Beth glances briefly at Sam before smoothing back the hair from her forehead. "Oh, it's just someone playing more tricks again."

"That's not playing, that's vandalism. How long has this been happening?" Sam looks steadily at her aunt, urging her to confide in them.

"I told you last night not to worry about it, Sam. Really, it's nothing your uncle and I can't handle. If I thought that it was serious, I would notify the police. But what would I tell them? I haven't seen anyone do the deeds, and I don't think they would believe me if I said a ghost was doing it. *I* wouldn't believe it." Beth looks down at her hands, trying to hide the lack of conviction on her face.

"You haven't reported *any* of this stuff to the police?" Sam asks, her expression incredulous. "I don't understand that."

"Well, we made reports the two times that tires were slashed. The car owners had to have a report for their insurance company. But the other stuff's all small things that are not even worth our home owner's deductible. It's cheaper to just replace those things ourselves. The police know about it, but not officially.

"Besides, you don't understand how things work in the small communities out here. If we reported all of the minor damage going on, it would only fuel the rumors and make our situation worse. Better to keep it to ourselves and not let the culprits get the attention they want."

Tapping the table in concentration, Sam thinks about what her aunt has said. Some of it makes sense. "What about a security camera?" she finally asks. "My dad got one last year to put over the garage. It's not that expensive."

"Your Uncle Bill already thought of that, Sam," Beth answers with a smile. "None of the local stores has what he wants, though, so it's on order. It should come in sometime next week."

"Well, good!" Sam is relieved they are at least doing that much. "If you need any help with things today, please let us know."

"Oh, no you don't!" Beth protests. "You girls are here to have fun, not to help run the inn. Why don't you go out to Florence Lake? It's about four miles round trip by the trail. You can even pack a picnic lunch if you like, and make a day of it. The trail is well groomed, so you can't get lost. It's one of my favorite places around here."

Sam and Ally smile at each other. "Aunt Beth, you must be a mind reader," Sam says. "We saw Florence Lake on our way up. I was going to ask if it would be okay to go explore it."

"Explore all you want! There's even a boat tied up to the dock at the end of the trail. I know you can row, Sam, but how about you, Ally?"

"My family has a canoe we take to the local lakes, so I learned how to row a long time ago."

"Good! Just be sure that you both put on a lifejacket. They're in the boat. That is a requirement. I trust that you will follow the rules, and be back before dinner so that I don't worry." She looks expectantly at Sam.

"Of course, Aunt Beth! I promise," Sam assures her.

After clearing the table and making a big lunch for later that afternoon, Sam and Ally head out into the warm, inviting morning.

6

FLORENCE LAKE

The boat that Beth mentioned turns out to be a very old rowboat that looks as if it might not float once they get in it. Emerging from the thick woods, they can't help but spot it right away.

"That's the boat?" Ally asks skeptically. Wiping her forehead, she sets down their lunch and pulls out two water bottles. It was a decent hike. Beth was right about the trail; it was clearly marked and impossible to miss.

Taking the water from Ally, Sam squints towards the weathered dock. An eagle calls out from overhead and she shifts her attention to the sky. The beauty of the place is breathtaking. Even from within the forest, they knew they were on special ground. Looking back at the water spread out before them, she tries to gauge how far across it is.

"That's got to be the boat," Sam finally says. "I don't see any other docks."

Florence Lake is bigger than it looked from the road last night. It's at least a good mile to the other side, and Sam can't even see the far end, which bends around to the right and out of sight. She'll have to ask her uncle about fishing. That would be fun.

"Well, let's at least check it out," Sam suggests, walking out onto the dock cautiously. "Aunt Beth wouldn't have told us to go out in it if it wasn't safe."

Upon closer inspection, they find that it is like the dock, weathered but sound. Four life vests are neatly tucked away in a center bench, and two sturdy oars are stowed in the bottom of the boat. "All it needs is a little paint!" Sam announces, smiling at Ally.

Ally doesn't look all that convinced as she gingerly climbs in, but the boat proves reliable as they put the oars in the locks and start rowing out to the center of the lake. It isn't a big boat, but it's wide enough that it isn't too wobbly and is easy to handle.

The sun is full upon their backs now as they sit facing each other. Sam rows backwards and Ally forwards, with the small bench in between them. Shards of light are reflected back at them off the deep, murky water in a dazzling display. The Rockies cut a jagged horizon in the distance, reminding them of their remoteness. They feel instantly cleansed of city life. The only sound other than the eagle is the splashing of the old wooden oars breaking the surface of the lake.

After about ten minutes of rowing, Sam and Ally decide to let the boat drift and share a can of pop.

"Wow!" Sam exclaims, after taking a long swallow and passing the can to Ally. "Have you ever seen anything more beautiful?"

Taking the offered can with one hand, Ally makes small swirls in the water with the other. *I think I'm already getting a blister,* she thinks, looking at the red marks on her fingers. "I have to admit," she answers, "I really am glad that I came, even though my phone doesn't work. Your aunt and uncle are wonderful and this might be more relaxing than a sunset on the-"

Ally's hand freezes above the water, and the pop can slips from her fingers, clinking into the bottom of the boat.

The clatter draws Sam from her daydream and she stares, puzzled, at the still form of her friend.

"What is it, Ally?" she asks quietly.

"I saw something, Sam," she whispers, pulling her hand into the boat. "Something big."

Sam sighs and tries to smile. "It was just a fish. I'm sure there are some big ones in here." But she isn't sure enough to convince even herself.

"It wasn't a fish!" Ally counters. "I know what a fish looks like, and they don't have rubber fins."

"Rubber fins? You mean like the kind you use for swimming? Who would be in the lake? No one else is here. This is on my aunt and uncle's property. It's not like there's a scuba shop nearby. It has to be something else. It's easy to see shapes-"

The right side of the boat suddenly rises up, as if a large swell hit it.

Sam realizes in shock that the boat is going to capsize. She hears a muffled scream of alarm as Ally plunges into the cold water, and then the bottom of the boat is on top of her!

****

The next few seconds fly by in a blur of confusion as Sam swims out from under the overturned boat and breaks through the water's surface. Her lifejacket has come off from the force of hitting the water. *That'll teach me not to simply slip it over my head without fastening the clasps*, she thinks, as she struggles to remain calm. Closing her eyes, she treads water and concentrates on breathing slowly. She's a very strong swimmer but open water has always freaked her out.

She can hear Ally calling to her, but fights to control her rising panic before responding, sure that at any moment something is going to grab her feet. She finally turns at the sound of splashing behind her and watches as Ally swims smoothly up to her. Thankfully, Ally's lifejacket is still on, and she has Sam's vest in one of her hands.

"Here, you lost something," Ally gasps, looking down into the dark water as they both float next to the upside-down boat.

"Thanks." Sam takes it gratefully. They are both good swimmers, but have enough sense to know they can't take chances this far from shore. "What in the world happened?" she asks Ally, hoping that she saw something.

"The only thing I know is that I want to get out of here now," Ally replies, grabbing a side of the boat. "There's no way we're going to get this boat turned back over out here, but we might be able to swim and pull it to shore. We aren't that far away."

"Yeah, okay…let's get out of here," Sam agrees as she quickly paddles to the opposite side of the boat. With some effort, they begin to swim for the dock. Within twenty minutes they reach their destination. After turning the boat upright, they collapse on the end of the pier, exhausted.

"Well, that was definitely *not* a fish," Ally says, stating the obvious. She sits up to wring the water out of her shirt. "Maybe we'll see whoever it was when they get out of the water."

"Not likely," Sam says, shaking her head. "There are hundreds of places along the shore where someone could climb out unnoticed. And something tells me whoever it was doesn't want to be seen."

"Sam, let's go back now." Ally suddenly realizes how serious the situation could have been. She nervously scans the lake while pulling her sopping wet old high tops back on, and stands up. "I think it's clear we're not wanted here."

"That's exactly why we're staying!" Sam says stubbornly. "Or at least until we're dry and have some lunch. Thank goodness we left our food on the dock!"

"I don't see how you can think of eating when someone just tried to drown us," Ally protests. But she bites into the ham sandwich Sam gives her and chews hungrily.

Within an hour, they are just about dry and heading back on the trail towards the inn. Ally has to walk quickly to keep up with Sam's fast pace. "Your aunt's going to flip when she finds out about this."

"No," Sam objects. "We aren't going to tell her anything except what a wonderful day we've had."

"Why not?" Ally asks, getting frustrated. "They need to *do* something, Sam, or at least know what someone did to us, even if it *does* mean having to go home. We need to think about what's best for your aunt and uncle, too."

"That's exactly why we aren't going to tell them," Sam explains, noting Ally's questioning look. "I think," Sam continues, "that whoever was in the lake is the same person who's 'haunting' the inn. They knew we had life vests on and weren't that far from shore. I don't think they meant us any real harm.

"Don't you see? They believe that by scaring us, they'll also scare Aunt Beth and Uncle Bill. And if they scare the guests, too, that could even bankrupt Hollow Inn. That must be their goal; they want my aunt and uncle to give up and leave."

"But who would do such a thing, and why?" Ally asks.

"The 'who', I don't know," Sam answers,

"but the why is pretty obvious. Someone is still trying to find Shawn Hollow's money."

"Of course!" Ally shouts, now seeing Sam's train of thought. "Without anyone around to get in their way, it would make hunting for it a lot easier. But what can *we* do?"

Sam stops in the middle of the forest path and faces Ally. "I'll tell you what we're *going* to do," she says defiantly. "We're going to find it first! And we'll start by reading that journal from cover to cover."

7

THE JOURNAL

Sam and Ally emerge from the woods at the edge of the clearing where Hollow Inn stands. They lingered on their way back so her aunt wouldn't wonder why they didn't stay at the lake longer. It's now about 4:30, and evening is drawing near. A breeze rustles through the many trees scattered on the slope in front of the big house, causing birds to take flight. A few land on the rim of a bronze bird bath with an angel in the middle.

"This is an incredible place, Ally. I won't let anyone steal it from them," Sam vows as they make their way towards the inn.

They walk slowly along a rock path, past the bird bath, and then a bungalow where the staff live. As they reach the back door of the inn, they smell onions frying and bread baking. Sam is thinking over the events of the day when they walk into the kitchen. She doesn't hear the question her aunt asks her.

"Sam," Beth repeats. "I said, 'how was the lake'?"

Sam snaps to attention and blushes. "Sorry, Aunt Beth," she apologizes. "I was just daydreaming about how beautiful this whole place is. I can see why you love it so much."

"Thank you, dear," Beth replies. "I take that to mean you had a nice time? Did you find the boat?"

"Oh, we found it all right!" Ally chirps, then stammers, "I mean, it was right where you said it would be." Before Beth can ask any more questions, the two girls excuse themselves and run upstairs, saying they need to change.

"Dinner will be ready in about forty-five minutes!" Beth calls after them.

"That was close!" Sam says, once they are in Ally's room.

"Yeah, sorry, I almost slipped. I'm just not used to keeping things from people. I hope you're right about not telling them."

"I'm sure I am," Sam assures her friend, as she passes through the connecting door and disappears into her own room. *At least I hope I am,* she thinks to herself.

Sighing, she picks up the old book. "I know there must be *something* in here about where the money is," she says out loud to no one in particular. Always eager to solve a mystery, this is the first time Sam has actually found one. The logical part of her brain says to go downstairs right now and tell her aunt what happened at the lake. But the adventurous spirit in her says otherwise.

"I have a feeling," she says softly to the diary in her hands, "that if you can tell us where the money is, we'll find our ghost. And I'm willing to bet that it's *not* Joseph Hollow."

***

Sam and Ally make it back downstairs in time to help set the big, formal dining room table. It's opposite the kitchen on the other side of the foyer and adjoins a large family room that they glimpsed last night. Just like the stairs, the table and all the original furniture in the other impressive room are made of a dark, rich oak.

Dinner consists of a large pot roast accompanied by all the traditional trimmings. The girls offered to help earlier, but Beth explained that they employed one maid to take care of cleaning the guest rooms and to help serve meals.

As they sit down to eat, Ted and the maid join the four of them. It's obvious immediately that Bill and Beth are well liked by their employees. As they exchange happy chatter, not one word of the "ghost," or the disabled lights is mentioned.

Sam is aching to get back upstairs to the journal, but she follows her uncle obligingly into the family room after supper. She is there to visit with them, after all. The mystery can wait for a little while.

Ted excuses himself for the evening, and the maid busies herself with clearing the table, flatly refusing any assistance from Sam and Ally. Bill lights a sweet-smelling pipe, taking Sam back to other nights of family gatherings.

"So, Sam," he says, "what do you think of the old place?"

"I was just telling Aunt Beth this afternoon how wonderful I think it is," she replies sincerely. "You've put a lot of work into it."

"Thank you so much for inviting us," Ally adds. "We're really enjoying ourselves." She glances guiltily at Sam, unnoticed by Mr. Clark.

"Well, I know there isn't that much to do around here." Bill stretches out on an old leather recliner and puts his feet up. "It's just a place to relax and enjoy nature."

"There's plenty to do," Sam tells him, taking a seat on the overstuffed couch. "You just have to know where to look."

"Fortunately, we know where some of those places are!" Beth says happily. "In fact, Ted has agreed to lead you on a hike tomorrow to one of the popular features, if you're interested."

"Of course we are!" Ally says, intrigued. "What is it?"

"Mr. Hollow named several natural formations after his family, like the lake," Beth explains. "One of them is a bluff that overlooks the valley. It's a ways to get to it, but a very nice hike. The property spreads out for almost two hundred acres, so you can go a long ways before you are actually lost!"

"Good thing I brought a compass with me then," Sam tells her. "I didn't realize it was that big!"

"If we can get things on track with the inn," Bill explains, "we want to build cabins down on the lake to rent out, a central hall for guest activities, and a small store."

"That sounds amazing!" Ally says. "My parents would love to stay at something like that. You could even rent out boats and maybe get some horses and do trail rides and…"

"Whoa…," Bill laughs, holding out his hands. "One hurdle at a time. First, we have to get past this whole legend thing and bring in some paying customers. Maybe if we can make it more than a couple days without stories about mysterious disruptions here, we'll be okay."

Sam and Ally look at each other, glad that they decided to keep the lake incident to themselves. If a story like that made it back to town, it would be hard to explain. It would be better to keep it under wraps until they figured out who was behind it.

"Have you seen these pictures before, Sam?"

Turning, she finds that her aunt has brought out a large photo album. Beth has it opened to some old pictures of Sam as a toddler. Laughing, she shakes her head and takes the album into her lap.

"Wow," Sam groans.

Ally scoots in close and the girls spend the next hour going through the whole album, talking about the family reunions and other events where the photos were taken.

When they get to the end, Aunt Beth puts the album away and tells the girls to follow her. Intrigued, they are led through a maze of rooms at the back of the house, until they eventually reach a small, neat library. There, Beth turns on the inn's only computer and invites them to get caught up with their friends.

Ally eagerly logs on to her favorite social media account, but soon discovers just how slow a dial-up modem is. After waiting nearly five minutes to load just one video, the girls quickly give up and turn the computer off. Sam is almost relieved, happy instead to explore some of the rooms before returning to where her aunt and uncle are.

Uncle Bill smiles when they enter the room, patting his generous stomach. "I'll take a big slice of that chocolate cake you've got stashed out there," he says eagerly to Aunt Beth.

"I'm sure you will!" she says, smiling broadly. "How about you girls?" she asks, heading for the kitchen. "Would you like a piece?"

Though it sounds good, Sam can't wait another minute to get upstairs. "None for me, thanks," she says quickly. "I'm pretty tired. I think I'll turn in early."

"Me too!" Ally adds.

"Well, I think that's a good idea," Beth agrees. "You'll need to be up bright and early tomorrow morning for your hike." They all exchange goodnights. Soon Sam and Ally are seated on Sam's bed, the journal between them.

"You read it," Ally says, folding her legs under her nightgown. "You're a much better reader than I am."

"Okay," Sam agrees, opening the old book to the first page. "Here goes!"

June 18, 1903

Well, I've finally done it! I've built the house of our dreams for my beautiful wife. Two years ago I felt that all was lost with the death of my brother in the mine. However, I have found a way to honor his memory by turning this property into something else.

We're set high up in the mountains, with our nearest neighbor ten miles away. If you look out the front yard, you can see a lake nestled in the woods. I'm naming this lake after Florence, since their beauty is comparable. When our children arrive I will in turn name a landmark after each of them, so our names will linger long after our souls are laid to rest."

"Geez," Ally sighs, "your aunt was right. Shawn really was a poetic writer."

"I'm more interested in the mine he mentioned," Sam states. "Is that how he got all his money? A gold mine?"

Hoping for more answers, Sam continues reading for another hour, but soon becomes discouraged. Most of the journal contains boring tales of kids doing unspectacular things and neighbors coming for visits. After skimming several more pages, she finally finds something fascinating:

November 15, 1924

Last week I hired a young girl from town to sit as a midwife with Florence. With the other three boys to look after and the property to manage, I just don't have the time for Florence. Nancy seems to be quite able as a midwife and she fits in very nicely. I'm already feeling a kind of kinship towards her. She was orphaned at the age of twelve and she says this is her first real home.

Sam closes the book and creases her brow. "This is almost where we were last night, when Florence dies. You'd think he would have said something about his money by now." Sam looks at her friend for confirmation.

"I suppose you're right," Ally admits, heading for her room. "If there really were something in there, I think the son who already found and read the book would have discovered what it was. Or whoever else has read it since then."

Trying not to give up hope, Sam picks up her cup of water off the nightstand and takes a long drink. Her throat is dry after reading out loud for so long. "Not necessarily," she calls to Ally in the other room, flipping through the pages with her other hand. "They might not have figured it out if it weren't obvious."

"Time for some fun!" Ally suddenly yells, appearing back at the door with two large pillows in her hands. Before Sam can tell her to wait, a pillow comes sailing and hits her square in the chest, knocking the glass from her hand.

"No!" she gasps, looking down in horror at the old journal in her lap, now soaked with water.

"I'm so sorry!" Ally cries, running to the bed, the other pillow falling to the floor.

"Quick, get me a towel or something!" Sam pleads, not knowing what else to do. Ally runs across the hall to the nearest bathroom and reappears with two towels and a washcloth, looking pale.

Sam has the journal open on the floor, desperately trying to mop the water off with the hem of her nightshirt. The old ink starts to smear, and tears spring to her eyes as the reality of the situation sets in.

Taking one of the towels from Ally, she presses down gently and blots at the paper, with better results. Taking several breaths, she tells herself not to freak out. Maybe it's just a few pages.

After some careful work, she gets to the back

cover. The inside is obviously hand sewn, with a yellowing, printed fabric tacked to some kind of board. The water has soaked through it, and Sam is afraid that it could fall apart if she touches it. It might be better to just let it dry.

Looking at it more carefully, she notices that the wet fabric has become transparent. Underneath is an unmistakable outline of a folded sheet of paper. "What's this?" she mutters softly, feeling along the slightly raised edge. "Ally, please go get me the scissors I saw on the dresser."

Confused, Ally does as she asks and finds the scissors next to the rest of a small manicure set. "What are you going to do?" she asks, handing them to Sam.

Without replying, Sam shoves a metal point into the sewn seam of the cover and quickly cuts the old fabric open.

8

A POEM

"What in the world!" Ally exclaims. "You don't have any right to do that! It's bad enough we spilled water on it. Have you gone crazy? Your aunt is going to…" She breaks off her complaints abruptly as Sam withdraws a yellowed, thankfully dry piece of paper from inside the journal's back cover.

"A map!" Sam practically yells. But her look of accomplishment turns to one of confusion as she carefully unfolds the document.

"What is it?" Ally asks, curious now, trying to peer over Sam's shoulder.

"Well, it's *not* a map," Sam says lamely. "It

looks like it's some sort of poem." She stares at it intensely for a minute, and then suddenly her face brightens again. "Ally," she says, "I was right in the first place! I mean, it's not the kind of map where 'X' marks the spot, but I think it tells us where the money is. Only...I can't figure it out."

"Read it to me!" Ally presses. "Maybe if we put our heads together, we can make some sense of it."

Nodding, Sam holds up the fragile piece of paper:

"My dear Florence, you have gone and taken with you my soul. So I will place my life's endeavors where forever, your beauty I'll hold.

I lay within a body of flight, and pray for my safe keeping. For in our sons, the taste of greed, in their veins is seeping.

The sun does set on your golden head and I watch, ever waiting. For the earth to move and us to meet, our love once again unabated."

"Now what can that possibly mean?" Sam asks Ally. "He says, 'my life's endeavors'. That has to be the money, obviously."

Ally takes the poem and looks it over. "I agree. But I can't figure it out, either. 'I lay within a body of flight.' What's that, a bird? I don't know where that could be."

"Tomorrow we'll look around the house," Sam says. "Maybe we'll see something that fits the description."

Ally looks skeptically at Sam, thinking. "Okay, but I don't know, Sam. Your aunt said that the property is nearly two hundred acres. There's no guarantee that the money is hidden *here*, in the house. His sons spent years looking for it before they died. It's been decades since he wrote that. Maybe whatever he's describing doesn't even exist anymore."

Sam has always appreciated the way her smart friend thinks about things. Ally is absolutely right, but Sam isn't about to give up.

"Maybe, Ally, but what if we *find* it? It would mean everything to my aunt and uncle. Not only would it prevent them from losing the inn, but they would be able to expand like they want to. Imagine how much fun it would be to come here next year and stay in a cabin on the lake!"

Smiling, Ally reads through the poem again. "It would be kinda cool if we figured it out. If we don't, though, we have to be sure and give this to your aunt."

"Oh, of course!" Sam replies, happy that Ally seems more interested now. "Even though they don't believe in it, it's still their property, so we have to give it to them. We'll just...use it for a little while first."

"You know, even though I'm going through phone withdrawals, I'm really glad I came," Ally confesses, handing the poem back. "To be honest with you, it's almost a relief to not have to be messaging people constantly."

Sam is surprised to hear this. She's always thought Ally loved texting and the social media stuff. Sam, on the other hand, often feels stressed out by it. It's good to know that she isn't the only one. "I know what you mean," she finally says. "At first it was fun, but now it's almost a burden at times. I feel like if I don't answer someone right away, or constantly share things about what I'm doing, people will think I'm weird."

"Seriously?" Ally asks hesitantly. "I didn't know you feel that way, Sam. We hardly talk anymore after school. I mean, we text and stuff, but it's not the same. Remember how we would always be on the phone or at each other's houses? It drove our parents crazy!"

Laughing, Sam takes Ally's hand and gives it a squeeze. "I know," she says. "Let's make a pact. Let's promise that from now on, we won't just text each other. If we want to talk, we'll actually *call*. I miss the way the things used to be, too."

Ally gives Sam a hug, then quickly grabs one of the dropped pillows. "I think we need to finish something," she says mischievously.

"Wait!" Sam hollers, as the pillow slams into her head. "No fair! I don't have one!" Careful to avoid the open journal and poem on the floor, Sam runs from her room and into Ally's. She arms herself with several more pillows from the big bed. For the next fifteen minutes, they act very much like the little girls they were just remembering.

That is, until Uncle Bill knocks on the door.

"Sam? Ally? Is everything okay?" Embarrassed, they drop their pillows. Sam looks at the clock on the nightstand next to Ally's bed and is shocked to see that it is nearly midnight.

"Sorry, Uncle Bill!" she calls softly. "We're okay. Just messing around. We're going to sleep now." They are answered by the sound of his heavy footsteps going back down the hallway. Looking at each other, they break out again in laughter, muffled by the pillows held to their faces.

They say goodnight and then go straight to bed. Back in her own room, Sam decides to leave the journal where it is, afraid to move it while it's still wet. The poem, however, she carefully refolds and hides in her bag.

"I knew you'd tell us," she whispers, zipping up the bag. "Now all I have to do is understand what you're saying."

9

CABIN IN THE WOODS

Morning arrives quickly. Both girls are still yawning while they walk behind Ted, following a trail of sunflower seed shells. The forest calls out to them as they go along the winding path, gradually climbing higher up the mountain. More than an hour has already elapsed since leaving the inn, but Ted has kept up a steady pace.

As they come to a level area, Sam has a chance to catch her breath and decides to ask Ted what he knows about the mine.

"I heard there used to be a mine here somewhere. Do you know anything about it?"

"Of course I do," Ted answers without

pause. "It's well-known around here as the biggest producing mine in the county."

"What?" Ally exclaims.

"I should say that it *used* to be," he continues. "Shawn and his brother were the first ones to mine the area, and the most successful. They had just hit a big vein of gold when there was a cave-in. Shawn survived, but his brother and two other men were buried alive."

"How horrible!" Sam cries, imagining what it must have been like.

"Shawn never recovered from the loss," Ted continues. "He used some of the gold to build the house for his wife...as far away from the mine as possible. No one ever saw the rest of the gold, though. Some people speculated that it never really existed, but I think his sons were right. They believed he just didn't want to spend the blood money, so he hid it away, instead."

"There!" Ted says suddenly, pointing across an open ravine to a large outcropping of rock on the opposite side. "That's called..."

"Why, that has to be Michael's Peak!" Ally announces.

"That's right," Ted confirms. "How did you

know that? I thought your aunt wanted it to be a surprise."

"We read about it in the-"

Ally stops as Sam jabs her with an elbow and gives her a disapproving look.

"The journal?" Ted asks, turning around to face them. "I didn't know that Shawn Hollow's journal was still around after all this time. No one besides his kids ever saw it, as far as I know."

"Um…yeah. Well, it was up in the attic," Sam says, reluctant to share the information. "It's just an old, dusty thing with a bunch of stories. My aunt and uncle haven't even read it." She tries to make it sound as boring as possible. The last thing she wants is for anyone else to get in on the hunt.

Sam almost walks into Ted's back as he comes to a sudden stop in front of her.

"Oh man, it's ten already!" he says, frowning as he looks at his watch. "I've got to start back. I know we originally planned a longer hike, but I've got some work that needs to get done this afternoon. If you want to keep going, just stay on this path and it'll take you around to the rock. It's roped off, and I would definitely stay inside the marked area. You kids have fun."

"Okay, I guess we'll see you later then," Sam says, her face burning at his comment. She hates to be called a kid; she's practically a teenager.

"Thank you, Ted!" Ally calls after him as he waves and disappears around a bend. As soon as he's out of sight, she turns to face Sam. "Why did you do that?" she demands, rubbing her sore ribs.

"I'm not so sure we can trust him," Sam explains, still staring at the empty trail. "I don't want *anyone* to know about this poem until we find out what it means." She pats the back pocket of her jeans. "We need to be the ones to solve this."

"He probably knows this property better than anyone," Ally counters. "Maybe he could help us."

"Oh my gosh!" Sam says, grabbing Ally's arm. "I just realized something! Now I *know* I don't trust him."

"What are you talking about?"

"We never said it was Shawn Hollow's journal. How did he know that?"

Ally crosses her arms, thinking about it. "He

probably just put one and one together. It's not like the journal's existence is a secret. It wouldn't be that hard to figure out. That doesn't prove anything."

"Maybe not," Sam confesses, "but from now on, let's be careful what we say when we're around him. Now, let's get over to that rock. I'm wondering if we can see the lake from there! We should look for carvings in it, too."

After another twenty minutes of walking, they reach the lookout and find that the view is breathtaking. They can't see the lake, but it's still spectacular. Getting down on their hands and knees, they examine the surface as far as they can but don't see anything that even comes close to resembling a bird…or any other kind of carving. Feeling let down, they break out the snacks they brought with them.

"Let's just go back," Sam says, stuffing their trash back in the bag. "Maybe we'll have time to check out the mine. I think that's going to be our best bet."

Gingerly picking their way back off the large rock, they reach the bottom and start back along the trail.

"Don't you think the mine would be a pretty obvious hiding place?" Ally cautions. "I'm sure that's one of the first places the sons would have looked."

"I guess," Sam says slowly, "but they wouldn't have had the clues that we do." She pauses, bending over and picking a blue bandana up off the ground. She holds it out for Ally to see. "Hmm, what's this?"

"Maybe Ted dropped it?" Ally suggests, taking it from Sam.

"No, he didn't have a bandana. I'm sure of it. It doesn't look like it's been out here for very long, either."

"One of the guests must have dropped it while hiking, then," Ally concludes, shrugging her shoulders. She starts walking again.

"Wait!" Sam calls out. "I think there's another trail here!"

Turning back, Ally goes to stand next to her friend, and they both examine the foliage where the scarf was lying. Sure enough, there appears to be a deer trail of some sort. Before Ally can object, Sam takes off down the path. "Let's find out where it goes!"

"Sam!" Ally cries, hesitating for a moment. When Sam disappears, she takes a deep breath and then quickly catches up to her.

Within minutes of following the narrow, winding path, they emerge into a small clearing. An old, dilapidated cabin sits on the edge of the open area. River rock from a crumbled chimney lies scattered on the ground. An old wooden door leans outward on rusted hinges, and bare holes gape where glass once formed windows.

"I'm not going in there!" Ally protests, anticipating Sam's intentions.

"Fine," Sam says, starting across the clearing. She disappears through the cabin door. It takes a moment for her eyes to adjust to the murky darkness, and what she sees quickens her pulse.

"Ally, come here!" she calls out.

Forgetting her uneasiness, Ally runs for the door, imagining all sorts of horrible things. When she gets there, she looks inside and lets out a sigh of relief. In a pile on the floor are fins, a face mask, and an air tank.

"So, *this* is our fish from the lake," Sam says. Looking around the small room, she confirms her suspicions. Stacked on precarious looking shelves are cans of food and supplies. A broken cot lies in the corner with moth-eaten blankets covering it, and a portable camp stove sits beside it. "Someone's living here," she says, stating the obvious.

The girls move back out into the daylight and inspect the woods around them cautiously.

"I suppose you're not going to tell your aunt about this, either," Ally complains.

"No." Sam confirms. Taking the poem out of her back pocket, she faces her friend. "Now that we have this, I *know* we can find the money. I'm sure this place is connected to the mysterious things going on. If my aunt finds out what happened at the lake, and about the person living here, our vacation will be cut short for sure, like tonight. Then who'll solve this riddle? No one! They don't believe there's anything hidden here. They wouldn't even look for it!"

Neither girl speaks for a while, until finally Ally nods her head. "I guess you're right. But Sam, this *is* trespassing. I know if this all isn't resolved soon, your aunt and uncle are going to be forced to sell. But this isn't something we can hide for very long. Let's agree to tell them everything if we don't find the money in a couple of days. Okay?"

"Agreed," Sam answers. "Two days. Now, let's get out of here before the person that stuff belongs to gets back."

As the girls make their way out of the clearing, they fail to see the eyes watching them from the woods.

10

CLUES

Sam and Ally arrive at the inn just in time for lunch. Keeping to their compromise, they mention nothing about the cabin or the diving gear. They find out that the maid has been given a couple of days off, since there aren't any guests registered for the rest of the week. They're happy to help out with whatever chores they can and eagerly go about cleaning up the lunch dishes.

"Aunt Beth," Sam begins, stacking plates into the dishwasher. "We read about a gold mine last night in the journal. It's somewhere here on the property, right?"

"Yes! I was going to suggest you go see that

tomorrow. It's at the very opposite end of the land. It's a good three miles each way, but there is an old gravel road that we've kept clear enough to use as a bike trail. We have several bikes here for guests, and I thought it would make for a fun ride."

"Would we be able to go today?" Ally asks.

Glancing up at the clock on the wall, Beth thinks about it for a minute, finally shaking her head. "I would prefer you wait and go in the morning. It's already after one and I don't want to take any chance of you not getting back before dark. There are all sorts of marked trails that branch off of it along the way. Knowing Sam, she's going to want to explore them all. I think you would have more fun if you weren't rushed for time."

"I think you're right, Aunt Beth," Sam agrees. "We were going to walk around the inn and the property near the house, if that's okay. There are all sorts of neat, old things."

Laughing, Beth dries her hands. "Of course it's okay. If you like antiques, there are enough in this old house to keep you entertained for a long time. I'll just need a little help around dinner time, but you're free until then!'"

"Thanks!" Hugging her aunt, Sam then starts for the stairs. Pausing, she turns back. "Umm... Aunt Beth? About the journal. Last night, I accidently spilled some water on it. I think it's okay, but some of the pages are damaged. I'm really sorry."

"Well, thank you for being honest with me, Sam. I'm really not concerned about it, though. You can even keep the shabby thing, if you'd like. I have no use for it."

Her face burning with shame over her aunt's compliment for honesty, Sam mutters a thank you and hurries after Ally. They both reach Sam's room at the same time and plop down on the bed. Taking the poem from her back pocket, Sam flattens it out on the comforter.

"'I will place my life's endeavors where forever your beauty I'll hold,'" she reads out loud. "This doesn't make any more sense now than it did last night," Sam complains.

"Let me see it," Ally says, taking the poem. "'The sun does set on your golden head as I watch, ever waiting.' Hey! Maybe there's an old picture of Florence somewhere, facing west."

"That's a better idea than I can come up with," Sam remarks. "I think I remember seeing some portraits in the family room. Let's start looking around there and work our way outside. We've got several hours still before it gets dark!"

On their way to the door, Sam glances at the nightstand where she left the journal that morning. "Ally!" she cries, "the journal is gone!"

Ally turns to the empty table that Sam is pointing at and stares in disbelief. "Are you sure you put it there?" she asks, opening the small drawer to double check.

"Of course I'm sure. The pages were dry this morning, so I closed it and put it back there. Oh, who would want to take it?"

"Someone who's looking for the same thing we are," Ally surmises.

"My aunt would've just asked for it," Sam ponders. "And Uncle Bill certainly wouldn't take it. That leaves just the maid and Ted. I'm pretty sure the maid left last night, though."

"Ted knew it was here," Ally says quietly. "I told him it was this morning. He sure seemed to be in a rush to get back here all of a sudden when we were hiking. I guess you were right, Sam."

"Wait a minute," Sam gasps. "It makes sense now."

"What does?" Ally asks.

"The first night we got here, remember how Ted helped my uncle carry his groceries in? Well, he must have seen us with the journal *then* and that's why he broke into my room that night to try and take it! When he confirmed this morning that we still had it, he saw his chance to try and get it again. I'll bet it was his plan all along to get us way out there on the trail, so he'd be sure to have time."

"But how did he get in?" Ally questions, looking skeptical. "The other night, I mean. Your uncle would have seen him in the hallway, and there isn't any other way he could have gone. I suppose today he could have just walked in, although your aunt would have wondered what he was doing."

"I'm not sure," Sam confesses, looking slowly around the room.

"How about the cabin, though?" Ally presses. "It would make sense to store some things there, but someone is obviously living in it."

Tapping her chin, Sam begins to walk along

the bedroom wall. "He must be working with someone," she says, distracted. "It couldn't have been him in the lake, anyway. He was here working on stuff around the inn all day."

Suddenly Sam drops to her knees near an old high-backed chair. "I knew it!" she shouts.

"What?" Ally asks, alarmed.

"That first night I heard a scraping sound. I assumed it was the door connecting our rooms, but we know he didn't come or go that way. Look at this chair," she instructs.

Ally comes to stand by her side, confused.

"See how far out from the wall it is? Look at the wooden floor. There are scrape marks under the chair, like it's been pushed back and forth several times."

Getting down on her knees now, too, Ally leans in close. "You're right! But why would someone be moving furniture in the dark?"

Grinning, Sam leans back on her heels. "Think about it. This is a really old house, designed and built by Shawn Hollow. Someone got in and out of this room without being seen. There's got to be a secret door here somewhere! Check the wood paneling behind it."

Caught up in the excitement now, Ally joins Sam in pushing on each panel of wood. She didn't even think it was odd that three of the walls were traditional, while this inner wall, the one opposite the connecting room, was done in panels.

"Oh!" Ally squeals.

Sam jumps back as the wall beneath her hands springs outward.

"There was a spring latch under it," Ally explains, as Sam moves the chair out of the way.

"I can't believe there's actually a secret passageway!" Sam says, her voice ragged with excitement. She peers into a long, dark hallway beyond the door and claps her hands together. "Maybe the money is back there!"

"I don't think so," the more rational-minded Ally replies. "Obviously, someone looking for the money has used this passageway several times, including when they tried to steal the journal. If the money were in there, I'm sure they would have found it."

"Oh, I guess you're right." Sam tries not to let hopes fall too far. "Well, that's okay. It's still really cool! Come on, let's get a flashlight and find out where this leads!"

Within minutes, they're back with a flashlight from the utility room and find themselves in the old, musty passageway. It's so narrow in between the walls, that they have to sit sideways.

"I'll bet I know where that goes!" Sam says after going a short distance. She's pointing at a door up ahead.

"Where?" Ally asks, as they stop in front of the old, ornate doorknob.

Sam pushes it open, revealing a massive bedroom with a huge four-poster bed.

"I'm willing to bet that this was Joseph Hollow's room. The same room where a 'figure' was seen looming over the bed," Sam explains.

They quietly close the door and continue their investigation of the passageway. A creaky flight of narrow steps takes them down to a back entrance by the root cellar. Not finding anything else of interest, they make their way back up the stairs and stop again at the secret door to the large bedroom.

"So this explains how someone took the journal without being seen, as well as the bumps in the night," Ally says. "But it doesn't tell us who did it, man or ghost."

"Maybe it does," Sam suggests.

Ally looks down at her friend crouched on the floor of the passageway. Sam picks something up and then stands, pointing the flashlight at the objects in the palm of her hand.

"Have you ever heard of a ghost that chews sunflower seeds?" she asks, displaying the empty shells in her hand. They are still damp.

11

A CONFESSION

Dinner that evening is served early. Like the night before, there is good food and friendly conversation. If anyone notices the knowing glances between Sam and Ally, nothing is said about their behavior. They have a plan brewing, and the time to pull it off is drawing close.

They spend the rest of the afternoon exploring the house, looking for old pictures or carvings. While they find some portraits and other interesting antiques, there isn't anything promising. They are both holding out hope for the mine the next day, because they're running out of ideas. Sam is very aware that she only has a day left before she's promised to tell her aunt and uncle everything.

After the dishes are cleared and the girls are done helping clean up, they use the phone in the front hall to call home and check in. Their parents are happy to hear from them, and Sam's older brother grills her with questions for nearly half an hour. After what seems like forever, they're able to say goodbye and then go outside to take a short walk before it gets too dark.

They paid careful attention earlier to find out what Ted was doing after dinner. They watched him leave the house a short time before to work on the sprinkling system back behind the house. Now they make their way in that general direction, keeping a row of trees in between them.

As they draw close, they begin their pre-arranged conversation, loud enough that he can hear it.

"Are you sure that poem you found tells us where the money is hidden?" Ally asks.

"It has to," Sam answers. "Why else would Shawn have written it? It's obvious that there's a message hidden in there somewhere. We just have to figure it out."

They pause with their backs to the trees, knowing Ted is crouched over a small trench in the ground on the other side. Sam hopes they aren't being too obvious, but it would be easy to miss him if you didn't know he was there.

"I just don't want it to disappear like the journal did," Sam continues, lowering her voice a little to make it sound more like a secret. "This time, I'll be sure to keep it hidden in my backpack. I wonder who could have taken it. Do you *really* think it could have been the ghost? Because that kind of freaks me out…" Sam can't help but smile at the last part, as they walk away and go back inside to wait.

****

"Do you think it worked?" Ally asks, sitting at the bedroom window. Peeking between the curtains, she tries to see if there is any movement in the gathering shadows between the staff lodge and inn.

"I don't know," Sam shrugs, pacing the floor. "I guess we'll find out in a little while. What time is it? It feels like we've been waiting forever!"

Pulling her almost-useless phone from her back pocket, Ally checks the time. "Nearly eleven," she announces. "We've been sitting up here for two hours now. Maybe he didn't fall for it. He seems pretty sma-"

Sam looks up to see what made Ally catch her breath. She is waving her over to the window. Making her way by the thin moonlight, Sam sits next to her and looks outside eagerly.

"There!" Ally says, bouncing up and down. "Over by the shed. See?"

Squinting, Sam watches the shed for a moment, and then tries to contain her excitement when she spots an unmistakable figure lurking slowly towards them. "Come on!" she whispers, pulling at Ally's arm.

Each holding on tight to a flashlight, they quietly enter the passageway. Moving to the door to Joseph's room, they sit facing each other, knees touching in the small space.

Moments after they get into position, the unmistakable creak of an old door is followed by heavy footsteps on the stairs below them. Although the person is moving slowly, it's impossible to be silent. When the approaching figure is only a few feet from them, they click on their lights simultaneously and flash them into Ted's stunned face.

First fear, then anger clouds Ted's handsome features as he tries to decide how to react. "What are you two doing here?" he demands hoarsely.

Sam rises slowly and looks him in the eye. "I think we should be asking *you* that question, Ted. Or should we just call you 'Mr. Ghost'?" she mocks.

"Okay," he admits, "so I'm guilty of making some noise. But I haven't done anything wrong."

"I'd call vandalism and causing some very nice people to lose all they've worked for very wrong," Ally chastises.

"I haven't done any damage around here!" Ted argues. "I sure didn't mean to hurt anyone," he adds quietly, looking down at his hands.

"Maybe you should be trying to convince my uncle," Sam says, turning to leave.

"No! Wait," Ted pleads. "Let me explain."

Sam turns back. After a moment of thought, she sits back down.

"Okay," she says, giving in. "But it better be

good."

"I guess it all depends on what you consider good," Ted replies. He sits next to them, their flashlights still playing on his face.

"When I was ten, I can remember sitting on my great-grandmother's lap, listening to her stories. One of them always stuck with me, and it's the reason I'm here.

"She told me about a kind-hearted man who took her in and gave her a home when no one else cared. She was only sixteen, and the man hired her as a midwife and nursemaid. She helped raise six younger foster brothers and sisters, so knew a bit about it. The man's wife died while giving birth, but my great-grandma ended up staying and helped to raise his four sons."

Ted pauses long enough for Sam and Ally to digest his story.

"You've read the journal," he continues, "so you know that I'm talking about Nancy. Shawn treated her like a daughter, and she loved him in the same way. It was very hard for her to leave. And when she heard he had died, she knew he died a lonely man.

"No matter how hard she tried, she could

never control Shawn's four boys. They seemed determined to make life hard for Shawn. He had spoiled them and they were very isolated up here. As they grew older, they didn't care about anything other than what they wanted, especially his gold. Great-grandmother Nancy said Shawn seemed more convinced as time went on that the boys shouldn't have it. He became paranoid and stopped what little banking he did and hid everything.

"He was always weird about the gold because of his brother's death. He would go into town a few times a year and cash some of it in to live off of. But, towards the end, he even stopped doing that. With the new will never getting to the lawyer, no one ever figured out where the gold was. My great-grandmother was sure, however, that it was somewhere here at Hollow Inn."

"So you *did* come here to take the money!" Sam interrupts angrily.

"It's not that way," Ted tries to explain, looking defiantly at Sam. "Last year, my parents were killed in a car accident. It wasn't until a few months later, with no family left, that I began thinking about Hollow Inn."

"I'm sorry about your family," Sam says gently, "but it still doesn't excuse what you've done."

"I haven't *done* anything!" Ted insists. "I don't need the blasted money. My parents' life insurance is all I'll ever need. I just couldn't get this place out of my head, or the idea of a treasure hunt. I needed something to do, a reason to go on, and I ended up here. When I arrived though, I found your aunt and uncle, Sam. I realized it wouldn't be easy to look for the money with people around. I was going to just rent a room for a while, but I'm not quite eighteen yet and don't have a credit card, or any adult to sign for me. When I found out they were looking to hire, all I had to do was forge a signature on my application. It's summer break, so your aunt and uncle weren't at all suspicious.

"I didn't have anything to go back to, nothing but an empty house full of memories. They really needed the help anyways and it gave me the perfect opportunity to snoop around. It almost felt like coming home, after all the years I heard and thought about the place."

"But what about the ghost?" Ally asks

tentatively.

"And let's not forget the vandalism, either. Or the fact that you tried to scare us with the legend on the first day we were here," Sam accuses.

"I may be responsible for the ghost noises," Ted admits. "It's kind of hard not to step on any creaking boards back here.

"The time when the guest found me in her room was a mistake. I was looking for the money, and I didn't realize there was anyone in there until she screamed. I almost left Hollow Inn after that, I felt so guilty. But I realized it would have made things even worse for your aunt and uncle, since they would have such a hard time replacing me.

"As for the damage," Ted continues, glancing at Sam, "I don't know anything about it. I've never broken a single thing, and I never would. I want to know who's doing it just as badly as you do. I told you about the legend and the ghosts because I felt guilty. I thought if I told you about it, you wouldn't suspect it was me."

"Do you know anything about the lake?" Ally asks.

"No," Ted answers. "What about the lake?"

"Nothing," Sam says a bit too quickly, looking sternly at Ally. Ted glances from Sam to Ally and back to Sam again.

"Sam," he says, "if something else has happened, you should tell me. We might be able to figure out what's going on."

Sam plays her flashlight along the passage wall, and then brings it to rest on Ted's face again. "There's really nothing else to talk about," she says firmly. "Except maybe why you stole the journal if your great-grandmother already told you everything?"

Ted's face flushes with anger, and he stands to go." First," he says stiffly, "I didn't steal it. I only borrowed it. You'll get it back tomorrow. Secondly, I'm not lying about anything. Nancy really was my great-grandmother. I wanted to read the journal for the same reason you did. I thought it might have some clue as to where the money is. Which reminds me, is there really some sort of riddle?"

When neither girl answers, he grins slightly and folds his arms in front of him. "Okay," he says, "I get the hint. No more questions. Just remember that I'm here, and I want to help you. But be careful. Somebody is causing that vandalism, and it's not me. Good night."

Before he can turn to go, Sam jumps up and grabs his arm. "Ted," she says, "I won't tell my uncle anything. For now."

"Thanks," he replies and disappears back down the passageway into the darkness.

12

GOLD MINE

"Don't you think you were a little mean to Ted?" Ally asks.

Sam and Ally are pedaling down a broad, gravel trail. Aunt Beth explained earlier that this used to be a road leading to the mine. They've kept it clear of weeds and put down gravel once a year to make a bike path. The mountain bikes the girls are now on are like new and handle the terrain easily.

Sam is trying not to get irritated. They had this same discussion last night after returning to the bedroom. "Ally," she says as pleasantly as possible, "like I explained last night, I'm not sure that we can trust him. I guess I might have been a little rude, but I don't think you can blame me. How do we know that he won't just take the money and run?"

"I don't think he would," Ally says with a surety that Sam doesn't understand. "I think we should have told him about the poem and what happened at the lake."

"Well, we're telling my aunt and uncle everything tomorrow, anyways, if we don't figure this out. I think it's better for them to decide what to do with Ted."

The two of them ride in silence for a while, taking in the scenery. They are traveling in the opposite direction of the lake and Michael's Rock. This side of the property climbs gently upwards with some nice level areas. The trail is lined with ponderosa pines and huge red cedars. Sam almost falls off her bike twice while tipping her head up to try to see the top of the trees.

It's another sunny, warm summer day, and the floor of the woods is slowly heating up, releasing its sweet scent of pine needles. It's a good smell, and it makes Sam smile in spite of the stress of the conversation. She hopes they'll find something at the mine. She doesn't really know what to expect, but her aunt made it sound like there wasn't too much to see. This was one site on the property not given a name. Shawn Hollow obviously didn't have fond memories of it.

"Sam, I'm sorry," Ally suddenly says.

Looking back at her friend, Sam sees that she is trying to catch up with her. She slows down, and they are soon side-by-side.

"I understand why you don't trust him. I guess I'm just kinda scared about everything and thought it would be nice to have some help. But we can do this on our own; I know we can figure it out!"

Encouraged by Ally's enthusiasm, Sam returns her smile, and they pick up the pace. They've already passed several smaller trails branching off the road, but they ignore them. They decided last night that they would wait to explore them on their way back. Getting to the mine and having plenty of time there is what's most important.

According to Aunt Beth, the road comes to a dead end at the mine, so it's impossible to get lost. It's about three miles each way, and they have already been riding for over half an hour. They should be there any minute. Just as Sam is finishing this thought, they come around a bend, and find themselves right in front of a rock wall.

"Wow," Ally breathes, coming to a skidding halt in the loose gravel. The face of the cliff climbs at least two hundred feet straight up, spreading to either side of them and disappearing from view into the forest. The entrance to the mine is about the size of a one-car garage door, with several boards secured across it. Off to one side is an old, weathered sign with the painted words 'Danger! Keep Out!' on it.

"Are you sure we should go in there?" Ally questions. She tries to peer into the darkness beyond the boards. "Your aunt was pretty clear about us staying out of it."

Sam struggles once again with her conscience. Ally is right. Aunt Beth told them they were absolutely *not*, under any circumstances, to go into the old mine. It wasn't stable and could have a cave-in at any time. Laying the bike down, she removes her backpack and fishes around for the flashlight she brought.

"We aren't really going to go *into* the mine," Sam counters. "We'll just check out the entrance. I'm sure that if this part weren't safe, it would have already collapsed. If Shawn hid the money in there, he wouldn't have put it deep inside where it might get buried. Don't you agree?"

Tapping her lip with a finger for a moment, Ally weighs the question. "I guess," she finally says. "But seriously, Sam, if we don't see something right away, I'm getting out of there!"

"Deal," Sam agrees, handing Ally a flashlight. Approaching the entrance with more confidence than she feels, Sam reads the other sign attached to the rock under the warning. "Established by Shawn Hollow in 1898. Closed in 1901 after the tragic deaths of three men that still lie within."

"Well, that's creepy," Ally says, looking around at the woods. They are basically in the middle of nowhere, and she reaches out of habit for the now dead cell phone in her back pocket.

"Could you imagine what it must have been like?" Sam asks, not noticing how uneasy Ally is. "The miners must have used horses and carriages back then, and had lanterns for light. Oh, look at this stuff!" She points out some antique pick axes and shovels arranged near the entrance. "They must have used some of these tools to find the gold. How cool is that?"

Ally tries to seem interested, but can't help being drawn back to the danger sign. The thought of the dead miners still in there somewhere overrides any excitement. "Let's just get this over with," she says through gritted teeth.

Sam locates a space between the boards that is big enough to wiggle through easily. Once on the other side though, her bravery falters.

Ally finds her hovering near the entrance, standing in the thin rays of sunlight filtering through the boards.

They both hesitate as they step into the heavy gloom. The air feels damp and smells musty, like an old basement. The flashlights do little to push the shadows back, as if the darkness is denser than normal.

"I don't like it in here at all, Sam. Can we please just go?"

Taking a deep breath, Sam turns to examine the rock walls on either side of them. "Let's just look for a few minutes, Ally. Then we'll leave, I promise."

They soon discover all sorts of sketchings and games scrawled on the walls, likely made by miners trying to pass the time. Distracted with their search, the girls end up a good twenty feet from the entrance, nearing the first bend. The tunnel has gotten wider and is littered with boulders and dust.

"Sam," Ally cautions, "we're going too far. We should go back now. I don't think there's anything here."

"I just want to see what's around this curve, and then we'll leave," Sam replies. "Come on! There are some pretty interesting drawings on here. One of these guys was quite an artist. I want to make sure there isn't one of Florence."

Ally follows reluctantly, shining her light over the rough stone. They've only gone a few feet more when the unmistakable sound of a rattle erupts from behind them. Spinning back towards the entrance, Sam searches the floor and spots a large rattlesnake coiled up in the middle of the tunnel!

Screaming, Ally jumps behind Sam, both of them retreating farther into the mine. "Is that a rattlesnake?" she cries, holding on tight to Sam's arms.

"Yeah," Sam confirms. "I saw one once before that was ran over in the road. They're pretty common out here. This one must have been under one of those rocks. Maybe if we just stay still long enough, it'll go back." In spite of them not moving, the snake slowly starts to uncoil and move towards them.

"What are we going to do?" Ally pleads. "We can't go any farther into the mine. It's too dangerous!"

Just then, another noise fills the tight space, coming from the entrance. It begins as a banging sound, then becomes footsteps pounding the dirt. As the snake is almost within striking distance, Ted appears behind it, one of the old pick axes in his hands.

"Get back!" he orders, raising the axe over his head. The girls do what they're told and move back several more feet.

In one swift motion, Ted brings the axe down and chops off the rattler's head. Even though the snake is obviously dead, he cautiously moves the head off to the side with the pick. "They can still bite you," he explains.

"Eww!" Ally moans, gingerly stepping around the rest of the snake and hurrying for the exit, Sam right behind her. They are soon standing back out in the bright daylight, the quick exit made easier by another missing board that Ted ripped off on his way in.

Following close behind, Ted emerges from the mine and stands glowering at them. "What in the world were you doing in there? Are you crazy? You could have been killed!"

Ally starts to cry softly, but Sam sticks her chin out. "We were just exploring. We didn't go that far. Who could have known that a *snake* might be in there?"

"Anyone with common sense!" he says, pointing a finger angrily at Sam. "Snakes love to hang out in caves, and no one has been in there for years. For some very good reasons. If the snake didn't kill you, a cave-in might have! Do you know how mad your aunt would be if she found out what you did?"

"Oh, please don't tell her!" Ally begs. "She'll be sure to send us home. Then we'd never find the money!"

"Thank you for helping us, Ted," Sam adds,

hanging her head. "We really didn't think it would be that dangerous."

"Exactly. You didn't *think*. If you're determined to go on this treasure hunt without me, do me a favor--try not to do anything else so *stupid*. Okay? I might not be there next time." With that, he stomps away.

Sam's face burns with embarrassment and for the first time, she begins to doubt that they'll ever find the gold.

13

DISCOVERY

"I feel just awful," Ally says quietly. They've been walking their bikes in silence for over a mile now. Neither of them are in a hurry to get back to the inn. After replacing the boards over the entrance as best they could, they'd gathered up their things and eaten their lunch before heading out.

"I know. I do too," Sam agrees. "I'm sorry for dragging you in there. You didn't even want to do it. I should have listened to you."

"It's okay," Ally sighs. "You couldn't have known about the snake. I meant about Ted."

"Oh," Sam says, surprised. "I'm obviously glad that he was there and helped us, but haven't you wondered *why* he was there?"

Stopping, Ally turns to look at her friend. "What do you mean?"

"Why did he follow us? He must have been spying on us, hoping to catch us finding the money. I think it's creepy, and I still don't trust him."

"But he helped us," Ally insists.

"Only because our lives were in danger," Sam points out. "It's not that I think he's evil, Ally, but I don't trust his intentions when it comes to my aunt and uncle and this property. I still think he's got to be working with the person hiding in that cabin."

"I think that the gold is making *you* paranoid now," Ally suggests.

Sam considers this and then shakes her head. "Maybe," she answers, "but one thing is for sure: things have gone too far. You were right. I should have told my aunt and uncle all of it from the beginning. It was wrong of me to drag you into this. We'll tell them everything tonight after dinner, okay? I'm really sorry, Ally."

Letting her bike fall, Ally turns and hugs her friend. "It's okay, Sam. Really, it is. Except for that snake, this has been really fun. I hope they aren't too mad at us and let us come back next summer."

Hugging her back, Sam is glad that Ally is so forgiving. "Oh, I don't think they'll be too upset. Except at the snake and whoever tipped the boat. I'm sure we can come back, so long as they still own it."

With that sobering thought, they pick the bikes back up and ride until they reach the open grounds of the estate. They head for the shed where the bikes are stored. After securing them, they go find Aunt Beth and insist that she give them some chores to do. Reluctant at first, she finally admits she could use some help with the laundry, since she changes all the bedding in the inn once a week, even if it hasn't been used.

Carefully avoiding any questions about the mine, the girls spend the next several hours washing and folding sheets and blankets. With the last bed made, Sam and Ally head back outside for a walk before dinner. They're both feeling anxious about the conversation they plan on having later.

Walking up the long, sloping back lawn, they

find an old iron bench at the edge of the woods. It faces the lake that sits in the valley spread out below them. Sitting next to Ally, Sam pulls the poem out of her pocket and sighs. "I guess we'll never know what Shawn was trying to tell us."

Putting an arm around her friend's shoulders, Ally tries to cheer her up. "Sam, look at the sunset. It's beautiful! It's reflecting off Florence Lake as if it were glass."

Sam starts to lift her head and then freezes, her eyes widening. "Ally!" she exclaims, "You're a genius!" Jumping up, she opens the sheet of paper and looks over the poem.

"What are you talking about?" Ally asks, confused.

"Listen to this," Sam says. "'My dear Florence, you have gone and taken with you my soul. So I will place my life's endeavors where forever, your beauty I'll hold. I lay within a body of flight and pray for my safe keeping.'"

Waving a hand out in front of them, Sam nearly jumps up and down. "Look down in the yard, Ally! What do you see?"

Ally follows Sam's gaze and studies the sweeping yard in front of them. "A bird bath," she answers.

Sam rolls her eyes. "What's *in* the bird bath?" she presses.

"An angel," Ally replies. Now her eyes widen, too. "A body of flight!" she whispers.

"Right!" Sam cheers. "Okay, listen, I'm not done. Here's the rest: 'For in our sons, the taste of greed, in their veins is seeping. The sun does set on your golden head and I watch, ever waiting…'"

"Florence Lake!" Ally interrupts. "The angel is facing Florence Lake!"

"Right again," Sam answers.

"So the money must be in the angel?" Ally whispers, looking around them.

"Yeah, I think it *has* to be! It's perfect," Sam replies.

"Well, let's go!" Ally says, and starts to run down the long lawn.

"Wait!" Sam cries, catching up to her and grabbing her arm.

Almost falling, Ally spins around and faces Sam, surprised.

"We can't just march up there and pull the angel apart in front of *everyone*," Sam insists, pointing towards the line of trees where Ted was again working on the sprinkler system. "Who knows who else is watching?" she presses.

"We could just go tell your uncle," Ally recommends. "Let *him* decide."

"You know he doesn't believe in any of this!" Sam looks desperate now. "He would probably take the journal and poem, and send us home tomorrow. Then we'd never figure it out!"

"What do you want to do? We've already agreed to tell them tonight, anyways."

"That was *before* we knew where the gold was!" Sam insists.

Ally frowns and starts to walk away, but Sam takes her by the arm again.

"Wait, Ally, we're still going to tell them! Just not right after dinner, but later tonight. After it gets dark, we'll have a chance to get the gold without anyone else seeing us. Once we *have* it, they'll have no choice but to believe us! Then they'll understand why we did everything. I think that it's the only way to save the inn."

Ally hesitates. Sam makes a pretty convincing argument. "I guess a few hours aren't going to really make a difference," she finally agrees.

Sam sighs with relief.

"But," Ally continues, "no more delays. If the gold isn't there, we tell them, no matter what. We have to confess everything."

"Okay, Ally. No matter what, we tell them. But I'm sure that the gold is there. It has to be!"

14

NARROW ESCAPE

The hidden door next to the cellar slowly opens, and Sam and Ally emerge into the shadows at the back of the house. They switch off their lights just as a cloud drifts over the moon.

"Can't we leave them on part way there?" Ally pleads.

"No way!" Sam says with determination. "Someone might see us."

They creep closer to each other and turn in the direction of the bird bath.

"Here comes the moon again," Sam points out. "We can see well enough to get there." Their heartbeats accelerating with each step, it takes several painfully long minutes before they reach the sculpture.

The bird bath is made of cast bronze and stands a good three feet high. The angel, also made of bronze, sits in the middle. It rises another two feet, so that Sam is almost eye-level with it. She begins looking it over as carefully as she can in the moonlight, pulling on each wing and tugging at the halo. Nothing seems to be loose.

"The head," Ally says from behind her.

Sam jumps, turning to look at her friend, a shadow among shadows. "What do you mean?" she whispers. "It seems solid."

"Try twisting it," Ally suggests.

"Twist the head," Sam murmurs to herself as she places her hands on either side. At first, nothing happens, but then she feels a slight scraping of metal on metal. "Ally!" she cries, "you've done it again! Here...help me. I don't think I can get it off by myself."

Both girls position themselves precariously on either side of the bowl of water, stretching out as far as they can to grip the angel's head between them. Working together, they are soon rewarded with an audible click and they are able to lift the loose head away from its body. It's so heavy that they almost drop it, but they manage to move it to the side and set it in the grass.

Hurrying back to the headless statue, Sam turns on her flashlight to reveal what was underneath. Nothing. Other than the threaded sides where the head screwed on, there is nothing but solid bronze. "Oh no," she moans, slumping to the base of the statue. "There isn't anything there!"

Ally's light comes to life and then bobs quickly up and down. "Sam! Come here! I think there's a lid!"

Sam crawls over to her friend and inspects the underside of the head. Sure enough, there's a cap, which she quickly unscrews. Letting out whoops of victory, the two girls look at each other, eyes wide.

"We've done it, Ally!" Sam cries.

Inside is a medium sized cloth bag, tied at the top. It takes up the whole space, almost as if it were molded to fit there. Pulling it out, Sam is surprised at its weight. Growing more excited by the second, she eagerly unties the cord, working the knots with trembling fingers. "It's coming loose," she breathes, and then the cloth falls away to reveal a huge clump of gold with a rolled up piece of paper on top.

"Oh!" Sam gasps, falling back on her heels. "This has to be at least twenty pounds of pure gold! How much do you think it's worth?"

"I'd say over half a million dollars," a deep voice says out of the darkness behind them.

Sam swings her light around, revealing a large, middle-aged man she's never seen before. He wears an old stained undershirt and his face is covered with stubble the same shade as his stringy brown hair.

"Very nice job, girls," he snarls. "I would have never guessed to look in there. But then, I didn't have the riddle did I?"

Sam lets out a cry of alarm as she realizes the man is holding a gun in his right hand. He motions to them with his left.

"Just give me that bag there, young lady, and we'll forget that this ever happened."

"No!" Sam says, her voice more courageous than she feels. "This belongs to my aunt and uncle now, and you have no right to it!"

"Don't you get smart with me!" The man waves the gun menacingly. "I've been looking for that for nearly *three* years and nobody, especially a little snot-nosed Girl Scout, is going to keep it from me. Now hand it over!"

Just as Sam is trying to decide whether to persist or not, a board suddenly whizzes though the air, coming down hard on the man's back.

"Oomph!" he curses, stumbling forward. Sam and Ally duck out of the way, falling to the ground by the base of the bird bath.

Ted jumps beside the thief before the man can regain his balance, grabbing the wrist of his right hand. A shot rings out through the darkness as Ted knocks the gun away. Spinning back towards him, Ted faces his opponent. Although older, he is an even match for him and they circle each other slowly, looking for an advantage. Ted quickly lunges, lashing out, but the stranger blocks the solid blows and manages to throw him to the ground.

Sam jumps to her feet and leaps towards the gun lying in the grass. She's never handled one before, but she simply aims it at the sky and pulls the trigger. The shot echoes off the mountains and reverberates across Florence Lake. Both men, now rolling on the ground, freeze. Several lights come on up at the inn.

"Stop it!" Sam yells, still holding the gun, now pointed at the ground. "It's all over, whoever you are! You're not getting the gold, and nobody's going to get hurt." She looks worriedly at Ted, who is slowly rising from the ground. "Are you okay?"

"Yeah," he says, breathing hard. "Thanks."

Just then, the back door to the inn flies open and the porch light snaps on. Uncle Bill stomps out into the grass, a shotgun in his hands.

"What in tarnation is going on out here?" he demands, straining to see who is there.

"It's okay, Uncle Bill," Sam assures him, "but I think you better call the sheriff."

15

THE INHERITANCE

They all sit around the big kitchen table, sipping coffee or tea. All, that is, except for the stranger. He sits with his hands tied together, behind his back. Ted keeps eyeing him angrily, and Bill still has his shotgun leaning against the chair he sits in. The pistol rests on the table in front of Ted.

"The sheriff has been called," Beth states as she sits down with her tea. "It should take him less than half an hour to get here."

"In the meantime," Bill says, "I think you all have some explaining to do. Especially you, mister," he adds, pointing at the man next to him. "Let's start with who you are."

"I think I remember him," Beth says suddenly. "Don't you, Bill? He's the man we chased off the grounds when we first came here. He was a little cleaner and heavier back then, but I'm pretty sure it's him."

"I think you're right," Bill agrees. "Weren't you looking for Shawn Hollow's money?" he asks the disheveled man.

"Humph," the trespasser grumbles, not looking at anyone.

"Well, what are you doing back here?" Bill demands. "It's been over a year since we last chased you off."

"I don't think he ever left," Sam volunteers.

The man frowns at her as Sam shares her theory.

"Day before yesterday, after Ted left us on our hike, Ally and I found an old cabin. Inside was the gear he's been using to go diving in Florence Lake, and--"

"Whoa," Bill interrupts. "How do you know he's been diving in Florence Lake?"

Sam and Ally look at each other guiltily. Sam blushes.

"You see, Uncle Bill," Sam starts, "I'm afraid

we've been keeping a couple of things from you. When we were out on the lake, someone… well, now we know who, turned the boat over on us. At the time, all we saw were some flippers. I'm sorry we didn't tell you about it, but we decided that we were going to try and find Shawn Hollow's money and the 'ghost'. I was afraid that if we told you about the boat, you would send us home."

"You're probably right," Beth agrees, her lips pressed in a tight line.

Uncle Bill has crossed his arms and is studying his niece closely, waiting for her to finish.

"I understand now what you were doing in the lake," Sam says, looking at the disgruntled trespasser seated across from her. "You thought that Joseph drowned while looking for the money, so Florence Lake was the most likely place to find it."

The man shifts his weight uneasily in the chair and lowers his gaze, but remains silent.

"When we found the cabin the next day," Sam continues, "we put two and two together. We figured there was someone else here looking for the money and that they were also most likely the ghost." She looks over at Ted.

"So that's why you were so wary of sharing your secrets with me," Ted says. He turns to Beth and Bill. "You see, I haven't been straight with you either." He goes on to tell them his story, including being caught in the passageway while trying to take the riddle. "I'm really sorry if I scared your guests," he finishes sheepishly. "I didn't mean to, and I swear that I didn't cause any of the vandalism."

"And he saved our lives!" Ally adds.

This leads to more questions and the girls tell the story about the snake in the mine. Sam's guilt intensifies, and she tries to avoid looking at her uncle. Bill's scowl has been steadily deepening.

"What's this about a riddle?" Beth interjects, looking nervously at her husband.

"Oh!" Sam cries, relieved to have a diversion. "This was the most exciting part." She slowly unfolds the brittle paper and reads the riddle aloud. "So," she adds, "we eventually figured out that the angel in the bird bath was the 'body of flight' that faces Florence Lake. We just discovered that tonight when we saw the sun setting on the water. I promise we were going to tell you everything after we checked the statue."

Ally turns to Ted. "How did you know we would be there?"

"I didn't," he replies, "but I did know you were up to something. I just waited around outside to see if you would sneak off somewhere and then followed you. I was positive there was someone else here causing problems, and I didn't want you running into him."

"It's a good thing he did, Sam," Bill says sternly, "or we might not have such a happy ending. I have to say that I am disappointed in your lack of trust. Keeping something important from the adults responsible for your well-being is not the right thing to do, Samantha."

"I know," Sam says quietly, cringing at the use of her full name. She knows her uncle is mad. "I'm so sorry, Uncle Bill. I know it was wrong. I just wanted to help you keep the inn."

She then turns her attention to Ted, thanking him for his help.

Ted smiles at her, wanting to relieve some of her discomfort. "So, are you going to share your find with us?" he asks, pointing at the sack Sam is holding in her lap. "Or is that a secret, too?"

Grinning, Sam lifts it up with some effort and places it on the table with a loud thump. She swiftly pulls at the loose cords and exposes the gold within. Everyone gasps in response, including Sam, even though she's already seen it.

"Isn't it amazing?" she asks, her eyes sparkling. It wasn't a nice, smooth bar of gold like you see in the movies, but rather a large mass of cooled molten gold still containing swirls and bubbles. Shawn Hollow must have melted it down himself to fit into the head of the angel.

They all jump at a loud knock from the front door. Bill answers it and soon returns, followed by two deputy sheriffs.

"That's him," Bill states, pointing at the man with his hands tied. "I want him arrested for trespassing, and for threatening my niece with that gun!" He points at the revolver.

"Well, that's Billy Fisher!" the taller of the two officers declares. "I thought that he left these parts over a year ago."

"We did, too," Beth says. "I guess he's been living on our property this whole time."

"What in the world is *that?*" the second

deputy asks, staring at the gold on the table.

"That's what should belong to *me!*" Billy shouts, trying to rise from the chair. The deputies quickly restrain him and put him in handcuffs.

"The gold belonged to Shawn Hollow," Sam says, pulling the sack off the rest of the way. "I think that the paper Ally has will tell us who it rightfully belongs to now."

Ally looks down at the scroll in her hands as if just realizing it was there. Sam handed it to her after the fight broke out, before going for the gun. "Oh!" Ally says. "You mean, you think this is old Shawn's will?"

"Let's read it and find out!" Beth suggests, smiling now.

Ally unties the old ribbon wrapped around the scroll and cautiously unrolls the yellowing paper. Squinting, she strains to read the faded ink.

"'I, Shawn Hollow, being of sound mind, bequeath my land to my three eldest sons: Christopher, Michael and Thomas, in equal parts. To my youngest son, Joseph, I bequeath a sum of five thousand dollars which is held at the State Bank. I regret that he is then on his own. He knows the reasons for this.

"Lastly, I bequeath this precious metal, attained at such a high cost, to the only currently living person who didn't love me for my money. I am saddened to admit that it is not one of my own sons. The person I speak of doesn't live at Hollow Inn any longer, but I know that she is still alive. Her name is Nancy Baker. My lawyer will be provided with the information to contact her.

"'I am placing this new will, along with my life's endeavors, in a place where my sons will never look. Its location will be provided to my attorney so that at the time of my death it can be located and carried out. In the case of something unforeseen happening, I will also leave a poem in my journal.

"If the words on this page are being read, I cherish the voice that declares it, for it means that I am at long last with my Florence, and we are reunited once again. This is my last will and testament.'

"It's signed *Shawn Hollow*," Ally finishes, her eyes misty. There is a moment of silence as everyone in the room tries to figure out what it all means.

Sam is the first to get it. "Oh, my gosh!" she exclaims. Everyone turns to look at her expectantly.

"Ted!" Sam continues, "if this gold was left to Nancy, your great-grandmother, then it must belong to *you* now."

"Your great-grandmother must have willed her estate to your grandmother," Bill adds. "Who did your grandmother will her estate to?"

"My parents," Ted replies, and then slowly grins, although his eyes fill with tears. "And my parents left their estate to me."

"Then it *is* yours!" Aunt Beth says happily.

"But I don't want it," Ted says. To everyone's surprise except Sam, he calmly pushes the bag away. "Like I explained to Sam earlier, I don't need the money." With that, he takes the gold and turns, placing it in Bill's hands.

"What are you doing?" the older man asks, flabbergasted.

"I'm doing what my great-grandmother would have done," Ted says with confidence. "I don't need the money, but Hollow Inn does. She would want to see this place completely restored and being enjoyed, the way Shawn meant it to be. The gold is yours."

Aunt Beth and Uncle Bill are speechless.

16

GOING HOME

The greyhound bus pulls up to the old depot with a groan, letting out a plume of exhaust.

"Here it is," Ted announces. He lifts the suitcases and turns towards the two young girls standing next to him. The sun is beating down through a cloudless sky, once again heating the day into the nineties.

Sam looks regretfully at the bus and thinks about the warm goodbyes she and Ally exchanged earlier with her aunt and uncle. They were too busy with their multiple guests to drive them in themselves.

After the initial shock wore off, Uncle Bill

agreed to let them stay for the rest of their planned visit. Sam's parents weren't as easy to convince. She would be facing some stiff penalties when she got home, but it was all worth it.

As soon as word got out about what happened at Hollow Inn, the media was all over it. Within a couple of days, rooms were being booked. Everyone wanted in on the nostalgia of a long-lost will, hidden treasure, and ghosts. For the past week, the girls have helped prepare the inn for the new guests.

Uncle Bill and Ted devised a way to make the hidden cabin part of a "Hollow Inn Tour," a loop of the property that will include all of the landmarks and key points to the Hollow story.

The maid returned to work the day after Billy Fisher was caught. And, with all the upcoming guests, they already need to hire another one, as well as someone else to help organize tours and other outings.

Uncle Bill made arrangements to meet with a local architect and contractor to start on the renovation plans. Sam and Ally can hardly wait to return the following summer to see what they come up with.

Even with the flurry of activity, the girls managed to spend many hours down at Florence Lake. With the threat gone, they were able to enjoy the amazing beach and water. Aunt Beth even went swimming with them, and Uncle Bill showed them all the best places to fish. Ted turned out to be a really good rower and took them all the way to the other side of Florence Lake, where they spent a whole afternoon exploring.

Now, ready to board the bus, Sam sighs and wipes her hot forehead. "It's hard to believe we've already been here for two weeks."

"I know," Ally agrees. "It seems like we just got here. I'm glad that everything turned out so well."

"If it weren't for you two," Ted says, "I don't think that gold would have ever been found."

"You would have figured it out if you had gotten the journal and the riddle before us," Sam says modestly.

"You don't give yourself enough credit," Ted counters. "You accomplished in four days what everyone else has been trying to do for years."

Sam and Ally both blush as they mount the steps to the bus. The driver takes the bags from Ted and packs them in the compartments above the seats at the very back of the bus.

"Looks like we're the only passengers," Sam observes, changing the subject.

"Good," Ally answers. "Maybe I can get some sleep on the way home." Stretching out across the back seat, she struggles to find a comfortable position.

"I can't believe how fast the inn booked up," Sam says to Ted as she takes her backpack from him.

"Yeah, I don't think they're going to have to worry for a while. Especially not after what the appraiser said about the gold. They should be able to do everything they want to and have some left over."

"Thank you for everything you did, Ted. Not many people would have been so generous."

"But I had to," he answers, grinning, "or I think my great-grandmother's ghost would have started haunting *me*!" All three of them laugh and Ted turns to go. "Now you better come back next summer," he says, pausing at the door.

"Oh, we will," Sam replies. As Ted disappears, she forces a cheerful wave and settles down on the seat next to Ally, who looks on the verge of crying.

"Ally," she says, tilting her head and looking at her friend with mock surprise. "I can't believe you!"

"What?" Ally asks, confused.

"We've been in cell service range for at least ten or fifteen minutes, and you haven't even turned your phone on, yet! What's wrong with you?"

Laughing, Ally hugs her best friend and then lies back down, with her head on her backpack. "I think…I might wait a little longer. I guess I've gotten used to not always talking with everyone. I kind of like it."

Smiling, Sam turns to look out the window as the bus begins to pull away. The station wagon is already headed down the road, into the valley and back to Hollow Inn. The mountains tower above it.

I know I'll come back here again, she thinks as the bus turns in the opposite direction. *In fact, nothing could keep me from it.* "Unless," she whispers aloud, sitting up straight with a smile, "I find another mystery to solve!"

The End

I hope that you enjoyed, The Mystery of Hollow Inn! Please take a moment to leave a review at:
http://www.amazon.com/dp/B00HMYJRZQ

Want to be notified when Tara releases a new novel? Sign up now for her newsletter! eepurl.com/bzdHA5

ABOUT THE AUTHOR

Author Tara Ellis lives in a small town in beautiful Washington State, in the Pacific Northwest. She enjoys the quiet lifestyle with her two teenage kids, and several dogs. Tara was a firefighter/EMT, and worked in the medical field for many years. She now concentrates on family, photography, and writing middle grade and young adult novels.

Visit her author page on Amazon to find all of her books!

Made in the USA
San Bernardino, CA
03 December 2016